SCARLET

BY

ARIA COLE

Beau Loup's world is taken by storm when Scarlet Fair appears in his life.

Her wild red hair haunts his thoughts and her luscious body makes his blood hum with life. She's the first woman to break him of his self-imposed seclusion to make him feel things he never dreamed possible. But she's all wrong for him.

Private schools and garden parties fill the world Scarlet lives in, and Beau is a rough man with a craving that consumes. When he realizes she may be the only woman with the ability to soften his hard edges, he's determined to show her how a real man loves a woman, and then maybe he can convince her to stay for life. He'll do anything to be her everything and he's bent on making Little Red his. In his mind she already is.

Warning: What happens when the big, bad wolf meets the sweet, redhead of his dreams? Hold onto your panties because we're about to find out!

DEDICATION

This book is dedicated to two people. My heroes, the smuttiest safe beta readers I know, and to whom this book would be nothing without: Gi and Nichole, you are my rockstars! Thank you for all the love, dedication, support, and giggles!

ONE

Scarlet

I stepped off the train, nerves twisting in my stomach as I looked for a cab. I juggled the duffel on my shoulder and swiped at the sticky heat dampening my forehead. It'd been a few years since I'd been to Gran's house, summer jobs and studies taking up most of my time these days, but when she'd fallen sick, I knew I had to see her.

I'd dropped everything and cleared my schedule, determined to be there for her all summer. Her frail voice had insisted that she was fine, she didn't *need* any help, but I'd refused to hear otherwise. I'd missed her desperately, and I'd let life run away from me, forgetting what was really important. It was time I slowed down, appreciate the old home where I'd spent my childhood summers, and soak up all the love Gran had to give.

A yellow cab sped up to the curb, the driver getting out of the cab and coming around for my bags. I rattled off the address of the old estate before sliding into the back seat, the driver packing my bags in the trunk before getting behind the wheel.

"We'll be there in approximately twelve minutes, ma'am."

I shot him a smile. My whole body was drained, and my mind was exhausted, but still excitement coursed through me as all the joyful memories of childhood started to emerge.

My Gran, the greatest woman I know, ninety-two

years young and so full of life. Going to her house has always been one of my most favorite summer traditions, but now the idea of going there made me sick with grief and sadness. I was going to my grandmother's house to say goodbye before the cancer made her too frail and weak. I knew I shouldn't be so sad—she had a full life of utter joy— βυτ at one point, old age can't be kept at bay any longer. My grandmother was my best friend. She was a sassy, sweet soul, and I wanted to spend all the time possible with her before she was gone.

I glanced down at my lap, where I held a box of pastries purchased at a small Parisian bakery we both loved. My lips formed a smile as the memories of those Sundays, of spending hours in the kitchen secretly eating all these delicious baked confections, flooded my mind. The various flavors and types of pastry were to blame for the extra twenty pounds around my middle.

The car rolled to a stop, and the cab driver got out, opening my door for me. I stepped out onto the stone driveway and peered up at the beautiful brick building that housed so many of my favorite childhood memories. Large, creamy pillars decorated either side of the two-story entry, a wide wraparound porch inviting visitors to stay and have a cup of coffee while overlooking the beautiful, impeccably manicured landscape. The view was breathtaking. It was like looking at a priceless piece by Monet. It was captivating and breathtaking.

"Scarlet!" The excited call from Darla blared from the vast front door. Darla was in her late forties with flawless skin and a soft frame. Her smile was as bright as the sun on a hot summer day, and equally inviting. I ran to her and hugged her fiercely. I had always loved her and her vibrant personality. I had missed her almost as much as I missed Nana.

"Oh, my pretty girl, I have missed you so much. I see you brought some baked goodies. I've been watching my figure, but you know how I never could resist those sweets. I swear since working for your gran I've gained fifty pounds. She is going to be so happy to see you, darling. I think you are exactly what she needs to lift her spirit." Darla twisted a lock of my hair between her fingers. "You always had the most beautiful red curls. My sweet girl, how was your trip?"

"I've missed you, too, Darla. I may have brought some of those apple turnovers you love so much," I whispered conspiratorially.

"This is going to be such a fantastic summer. Oh, and wait till you see the new looker that works for your gran. If only I was a few years younger." She chuckled, and her deep laugh bounced merrily off the walls. When Darla laughed, the world took notice. Like Santa Claus at the mall with a young child on his lap, her laugh was pure joy.

I found it a little sad that Gran hadn't greeted me upon my arrival. That she wasn't here hugging and kissing me meant only one thing: her illness had gotten worse, and now she couldn't physically afford to disobey her doctor. At least I had Darla to make me feel a little more at home. "How is she, Darla?" My voice was laced with sadness and worry.

"She has good days and bad ones. But she is still just as feisty and fiery." Darla smiled and winked at me as her eyes twinkled with mischief. Even though Darla was making light of the situation, I knew it was only for my benefit. It was a ruse to keep my spirits up.

* * *

After putting away my clothes and washing up in the bathroom after the long train ride, I wandered into the large bedroom that was still a shrine to my childhood, Gran had everything from my childhood out for display. I smiled that everything had remained as I left it, the only thing that changed was my single bed was now upgraded to an opulent king-sized version. I smiled, looking at all the trinkets from my childhood. Gran sure was teetering on borderline hoarder. I smiled cherishing all the love and devotion my Gran felt toward me, my whole life she had been my biggest champion and supporter.

By afternoon, I was disappointed that I had yet to see Gran, but Darla had told me that she slept a lot now due to the medication the doctors had given her. I decided to take a walk around the grounds to dispel me from my dark thoughts and look at the new beautiful landscaping. Whoever the new landscaper was, he had a very detailed eye. Everything was beautiful and perfectly arranged.

I felt a pang of guilt that I hadn't seen all this in the past years. My friends, school, and summer activities became more important at times, and my family took a backseat. You only realize the mistakes you are making when it's too late. I trailed my fingertips over the perfectly manicured hedge. I turned the corner and ran right into what seemed to be a wall but was, in fact, a giant, burly man. I stumbled, my arms thrusting out, and was about to fall flat on my behind when suddenly, two strong, rock-solid arms surrounded me. They wrapped around my waist, and stunning green eyes pierced right through me before his lips parted and he breathed, "Are you okay?" His deep voice pounded through my ears, the sprinkling of an accent registering, and I remembered

Darla's comments about the French landscaper. My heart thundered as I lay speechless in his arms, swallowing the utter shock and surprise I felt. His dark emerald gaze held mine for another long beat, his touch on my body the only thing I could feel. I trembled with the new sensations pulsing through me.

"Wow, your arms are huge…" I breathed and instantly wanted to go back in time a few minutes to erase the stupid words that had raced out of my mouth.

I was unable to say anything else, my eyes still trained on his.

His beautiful mouth curled into a crooked grin before his grip tightened around my waist and he hauled me against his body. "But they sure came in handy, didn't they?"

His words fell upon deaf ears. All I could think and feel was his body, this giant, stunning man holding me against him. His grip tightened again at that moment, almost taking my breath away. His presence was overwhelming, his broad shoulders and chiseled biceps stretching the thin fabric of his white T-shirt.

I'd never seen a man like this before. He was broad and formidable, and I felt remarkably small wrapped up in his arms. I peered up at his face, which was just as stunning as his stature. A dark, well-kept beard and nearly jet black hair had me aching to feel the strands beneath my fingers.

"I'm Beau Loup," he whispered as a small smile curved his lips. His words danced around the air between us, my mind too scattered at that moment to say anything profound.

"I am Scarlet Fair. My gran owns the house," I introduced myself, feeling his gaze flutter across my skin, setting it on fire as he went.

"Mm, glad to make your acquaintance, Ms. Fair." His gaze finally landed on mine again. His intense stare penetrating me to my very core. "I hope to see more of you." His words twisted in the wind, his tone and the wicked gleam in his eyes implying so much more. This man had a roguish charm about him, and if I wasn't careful, I would fall as his prey.

"Well, if you work here, it seems you will." I pulled from his embrace and missed the warmth instantly. Beau Loup didn't make me feel uncomfortable. Something about him was welcoming. Oddly enough, he reminded me of my father— big, rough, but completely kind-hearted.

"Work and live." His words pulled me from my thoughts.

"You *live* here?" I nearly swallowed my tongue.

His eyes rose in amusement before he answered. "I've got a place out back. Ms. Fair sold a corner lot to me a while ago."

I nodded slowly, my eyes tracing the stark lines of rigid muscle decorating his body. I could feel my face getting flushed.

I twisted my hands together, my skin prickling with aroused awareness. "It was nice to meet you, Beau. I hope to run into you again."

"I'm sure you will." He took my hand in his and lifted it to his lips. He placed a lingering kiss there, his gaze shooting a blaze of fire straight into my core, and his words hung in the air as he winked at me. Why wasn't he leaving? *Shoo, will you?* At that moment I didn't know what to do, but I knew I had to leave. This man had me trapped, and I needed to get out. "Well, I must be going." I quickly snatched my hand back from him and spun around so fast that I almost tripped. I noticed him lurch to catch me, and his face had lost that devastating smile, it now seemed to be marred with concern and worry. Just as quickly as that worry came, it vanished when he saw I hadn't fallen.

I swiftly ran off before I could embarrass myself any further. "Until next time, *petite rouge*." As the distance grew between us, I could still hear his laughter following me.

Sensations raced across my skin, curling my toes and prickling the hairs on the nape of my neck. The feeling of immediate danger seemed to course it's way through my body, as if raging and combusting in my bloodstream.

TWO

Beau

I normally didn't spend my days up at the big house—I hired people for the menial tasks—but today I needed to work with my hands.

I needed to feel tools in my hands, I loved crafting generic pieces of wood into something beautiful. It was a dream I had for as long as I can remember, to be an artist. The idea of taking something broken and showing its beauty again appealed to me, bringing old, neglected things back to life.

I also found I loved working with Ms. Fair. I'd been taking care of the grounds of the estate for a while now, starting with backbreaking labor before I'd gotten my own landscaping and design company off the ground. Ms. Fair had only recently begun to ask me to custom design pieces for the estate after seeing an old handmade rocking chair I had made sitting in the bed of my truck.

She often had sophisticated parties, with debutantes coming and going from the mansion, the wealthy women getting grabby and doe-eyed around me, acting out their sexy gardener fantasies, I had no doubt, but the gruff, cranky, overbearing asshole in me usually kept them at bay. But Scarlet wasn't like any of those women, actually, I've never met a woman like her before in my life. She was a shy little thing who made me want to play and protect, the red blush and that innocent look in her eyes were sexy as hell. I couldn't help smiling when she talked to me, I don't think I had never smiled that long in my entire life. She looked so…cute…standing there with flaming red hair all wild and that cute little blush. I'd chuckled when she said her name, Scarlet. It suited her so well. She seemed to burn with a red-hot fire in a small package. *Petite rouge.*

I thrust a hand through my hair, stalking off around the corner of the house, my mind still on the pretty little redheaded thing. I hadn't been with a woman in years, and in truth, I hadn't missed it much. Not until now.

I turned, about to grab the shovel I'd come for, when I caught a glimpse of the gorgeous little woman walking away shaking that hot little ass. I just wanted to take a bite out of it. Dammit, she was so sexy. If I wasn't careful, I would become consumed with having her in my bed and on my cock. I bet she would look so hot naked, all that milky white skin with the long fiery curls raging around her body.

If Scarlet didn't stay away from me, I would become consumed by her. There was something about her that made me lose all perspective. I wondered what she would sound like while I buried my tongue deep in her, tasting her sweetness, smelling her scent. I wanted my cock deep in her throat and then buried in what I envisaged was the sweetest pussy imaginable. I wanted her scent to surround me.

I groaned quietly, then stalked off in the other direction, taking the long way back to my project in the backyard just to avoid her. It seems I'd need to do a lot of avoiding the next few weeks if I was going to keep my hands off her. Just feeling her form pressed against mine had launched lust into my system like never before, she just looked so damn sweet and felt so incredibly soft.

After spending most of the day finishing up the brick patio, complete with hand-designed and carefully crafted furniture, I packed up my tools, eager to get home. I was desperate for a shower, layers of grime and sweat covering my skin, but a sense of satisfaction was embedded deep in my bones. Ms. Fair had given me free rein to design things the way I saw fit, which made me even more motivated to make sure things were made to perfection.

Working for her was a complete joy. She was so vibrant and full of life, and a part of me thought she was a little bit on the dirty old bird side. I swear I caught her checking out my ass on more than one occasion.

I dropped the bag of tools into my truck and headed for the front door. The lady of the house had told me to stop by after dinner, which was why I'd chosen to work right through it, before I stopped in to check the architectural plans she'd laid out for a greenhouse in the orchard.

I tapped on the door lightly before stepping in, having felt more than welcomed in all these years I'd been coming here. Ms. Fair had always been generous, and in some ways, I felt more at home here than anywhere else, she had a way of making someone feel really at ease.

I took a few tentative steps into the great foyer, peeking around an open doorway to find the formal dining room empty.

"Oh, I suppose you've come for the blueprints. Give me just a minute, Beau." Ms. Fair appeared out of another door, a small smile on her face as she shuffled through a small side table. "The patio looks gorgeous, even better than I'd envisioned." Though her body may look weak, her smile was strong, and her eyes still danced.

She passed me the roll of paper. "Thank you."

I nodded. "Hearing you say that makes all the hard work worth it. I think the hardwood you picked will weather nicely." I was caught off guard when Scarlet came around the corner, waves of her fiery hair falling over one shoulder. My brain automatically went to thoughts of how those locks would feel in my fist as I kissed her so hard I bruised her lips. Those lips could make a man fall to his knees begging to just get a taste.

"Oh, Scarlet, meet Beau Loup. He owns the company that maintains the grounds. He puts those muscles to good use taking care of this place." Ms. Fair's papery palm pressed at my forearm as she winked at her granddaughter.

"I've already had the pleasure of meeting your stunning granddaughter." I smiled at Scarlet, desperate to see the blush rise to her face. She was so adorable standing there, shuffling her feet. My smile got wider as I thought how much this sweet girl wanted to run for the hills with embarrassment.

"Mr. Loup was so kind to catch me when I stumbled." Scarlet's honeyed voice floated between us.

"As I said, it was my pleasure. It isn't every day that a guy can play a knight in shining armor."

"I was just headed for bed, these days take a lot out of me, but I was just telling Scarlet my plans for the greenhouse. I thought maybe you could show her our plans before you head off for the night?" The elder woman's warm eyes danced with mischief as she gazed up at me, batting her lashes. I smiled, thinking how she must have had men wrapped around her finger when she was young. She certainly had the charm now.

"Well..." I rubbed at the back of my neck, wondering what in the hell she was up to. I'd been working outside in the sun all day, probably stank like a pig and wasn't the most presentable to entertain her gorgeous granddaughter.

"I don't want to keep you out late, Mr. Loup. I'm positive you're tired from working all day and evening out in the sun." Scarlet's ocean-blue gaze locked on mine.

I think my heart nearly fell on the fucking floor. "No, it's no trouble at all." I squeezed the old woman's hand and placed a soft kiss on it.

"Thank you so much, Beau. I know she's in good hands." Ms. Fair patted my arm as Scarlet approached, the lavender scent of her hair filling my nostrils and making my cock stand at attention.

"Sure, not a problem. Have a good night." I nodded at her just as Scarlet slipped her hand through the crook of my elbow. Nerves popped and fizzled with her gentle touch, and it took everything in me not to pull her against my body and fuck her mouth with my tongue.

"Have a nice walk, loves," Ms. Fair called before heading up the stairs slowly, leaving me and her granddaughter alone.

"I appreciate you doing this, Mr. Loup."

Without saying a word, I opened the door, standing in a position that ensured she'd have to brush against me as she passed. As she walked by me to head outside, I felt her breast brush up against me, and I nearly lost my mind. I wondered if my presence affected her the way she affected me, one look at her and I could feel myself coming undone. "You can call me Beau, you know.

Actually, I think I would like to see my first name rolling off your tongue." I waggled my eyebrows suggestively, and suddenly the most beautiful thing happened…I saw her smile.

"Well, Beau, thank you for showing me—"

"It's completely my pleasure, *petite rouge*." My eyes crawled down her neck, landing at the soft V of her cleavage. Her full round tits begged for my hands, I wanted to palm them and taste her succulent pebbled nipples with my tongue. "Scarlet, it's really my pleasure, girls like you don't come by everyday. You are enchanting." I pressed a hand across her collarbone, trailing my fingertips at the hollow of her throat, delighting in the hot dew of her skin.

I turned to put the blueprints in my car, but when I turned back to look at her face, she was gone.

"Fuck!" I grunted, frantic to find her.

THREE

Scarlet

I sped down the damp grass, heading for the house and the comforting warmth of my bed. Beau Loup was the most striking, charming, terrifying man I'd ever met. I'd never before felt the things he'd just made me feel in the pit of my stomach.

I pushed a hand through my hair, finally feeling my heart calm enough to allow me to think rationally before I reached the house. I stopped at the newly remodeled patio, resting my eyes as I leaned against the weathered wooden bench and went over his words in my head.

I was curious about his past, his history on the estate. I made a mental note to probe Gran for some answers about the mysterious Beau Loup tomorrow.

I looked up at the sky, marveling at the thousands of stars sparkling in my vision, before I heard soft footsteps in the grass. Sheltered next to a tall juniper, I tucked myself into the branches hanging over the bench, trying everything I could to disappear as Beau approached the house. I watched him as he stalked by, the hard line of his jaw and ripped bulges of his biceps highlighted by the silvery moon.

He was devastatingly gorgeous, so rugged, and manly. I'd seen him pull up his shirt earlier while he drank from the water faucet, and my mouth was nearly salivating again at the memory. I was drawn to him, and as much as I wanted to deny it, I couldn't. He was larger than life and took up the space around him and swallowed all the air in the vicinity. When he was around, I felt powerless, like a deer caught in the headlights, frozen in place and too scared to move.

I sighed softly, shifting in the quiet night when Beau finally rounded the corner, and I was safe. He hadn't seen me, but strangely an unexpected wave of disappointment churned through me. Despite everything, Beau Loup had cast his spell on me.

I spent the next few mornings with thoughts of Beau floating weightlessly in my head but lying heavy in my heart. I couldn't get the flirty, sexy man off my mind. He'd been busy working on the greenhouse all hours of the day and hadn't been up to the big house since the night I freaked out and ran away from him. My thoughts had run wild in the hours since then, and I was more than a little ashamed that I'd taken to spending afternoons tucked up in my bedroom, trying to catch a glimpse of him working, from my perch high above the grounds.

Finally, after days of confinement in the house, I slipped out after dinner, dusk just kissing the horizon, and headed for a walk through Gran's glorious gardens. I did my best to avoid the orchard and headed the opposite way, sucking in the heady scent of lilacs, trailing my fingers along the rows of evergreens that lined one garden wall. My mind wandered to Beau. The warmth in his eyes from the first time we'd met haunted me. Despite his charming and rather cocky exterior, there seemed to be something deep lingering in his eyes. I wasn't the kind of girl that really craved a man, but the touch of his skin against mine made me feel differently. Made me feel like I'd never felt before. I kept walking, my mind drifting off to school girl fantasies of his broad body pushing against mine as he kissed me, the slow probe of his tongue working my mouth and sending my body into a blaze.

The garden path dipped to the right, and I was surprised to come across a small bubbling pond stocked with fish, a beautiful, intricately wrought wooden bench perched at one edge.

I smiled to myself as I took a seat and ran my hands along the wood grain, wondering if Beau had crafted this piece too, his hands working the wood until it shone with beauty and character. My heart flitted in excitement as I remembered the way his cocky grin lifted one corner of his mouth and his eyes twinkled in mischievous amusement. The low tenor of his voice never failed to send butterflies racing in my stomach, his words dampening my panties. I swallowed the excitement clutching at my throat and slowly pulled the thin fabric of my summer dress up my legs.

My hands slid up my thighs, and I worked the flesh in slow circles, inching higher until I reached the elastic of my underwear. I slipped a finger underneath the band and teased at the hot flesh, a soft sigh falling from my lips as my eyes fell closed and my thoughts fell on him.

"Beau..." I slipped another finger beneath my panties and dragged the digits through the slick flesh between my legs. "Beau!" I cried, arching my hips off the bench as I massaged my sensitive clit. The muscles in my body bunched tightly, and I bit down hard on my lip as I felt something slowly building in the far reaches of my body. Like a slow chugging locomotive, it gathered energy and strength until my fingertips sped on instinct and I pushed harder against the hot flesh, chasing the release.

"*Petite rouge.*" His growl hit my ears before my eyes fluttered open and I saw Beau Loup standing at my feet, eyes trained on my aroused body. "Jesus, aren't you the sexist thing I have ever seen?"

Beau closed the distance between us in a heartbeat, his body spreading over mine on the bench, one hand pushing into my thick hair, the other roaming my torso like he was looking for buried treasure. "Fuck, I can smell how turned on you are." He placed fevered kisses along my collarbone as his hand spread my thighs, nestling his body between my legs. "You are so beautiful, from the second I saw you I knew I had to have you." His gravelly tone sent shivers burning through my clit.

"Beau," I sighed when he flexed his rigid length against my center, only the flimsy barrier of fabric separating us.

"That's it, *ma petite rouge*, show me how I make this sweet body feel." His palm crawled up my throat and held my cheek in his grip before he licked across the seam of my lips with his deft tongue. A slow tremor ripped through my body, and I vaguely wondered if it was possible to have an orgasm without direct stimulation because I was pretty sure I just had from his tongue. "Tell me you want me, too. I need to know that." My eyes grew big at his words, as shallow breaths wracked my body. "I want to know that you need me, because if I don't have you soon, I will go out of my mind."

His eyes burned with warning. It was so intense, so raw, and so demanding. He knew he'd won. He had me in his grasp, and I had no choice but to surrender.

I shook my head as I held his gaze. "Yes," I whispered softly into the night, embarrassed by my need for him.

His nostrils flared at my words, and I instantly knew it was what he'd wanted to hear. His eyes darted up and down my body beneath him before he shook his head. "If you were mine, I wouldn't let you out of the house in this flimsy shit." He pulled the strap of my dress down and attacked my shoulder with his lips and tongue, nipping and kissing and tracing invisible lines with carnal sensuality. His teeth caressed my skin almost like a warning and making my body and mind ache for him. He hadn't known it then, but the moment his hands first made contact with my body, I was his.

"So sweet. Every inch of you drives me insane." He yanked down the neckline of my dress, releasing just enough of my breast to drive me wild without even exposing a nipple. His hands groped at my skin, his tongue lapping at the creamy flesh of my breast before he nipped, sending a delightful shiver coursing through me. He rolled my peaked nipple between his fingers over the thin cotton of my dress before his other hand trailed between my trembling thighs for the first time.

I felt the press of his hand on my mound, and I sighed, feeling like a goddess beneath his intoxicating touch. He slipped one finger beneath the elastic of my panties and made contact with my scorching hot flesh. Arousal pumped through my body as I arched, desperate for more. "I love that I do this to you. So wet for me," he chuckled, before one long finger slid through the seam of my pussy and stroked the sensitive nerves. I arched and moaned into the night as my orgasm began another slow build under his attentions.

"No." I shook my head hastily, desperate for more

touching and less talking.

"Ah, sweet girl. I bet you taste even sweeter than you look," were his last words before he buried his head between my thighs, the warmth of his breath against the cotton of my underwear. He pulled the elastic of one leg aside, exposing my hot core to the cool night air, before I felt one long, slow lick from his tongue. My hips bucked, and I would have tumbled if it hadn't been for his powerful hands locked at my thighs and holding me in place beneath him.

I couldn't move. I was subject to his every whim, helpless to the pleasure he was giving me, and still, it was the only place on earth I wanted to be. My mind fogged with lust as his fingers teased at my entrance, his tongue fucking my clit in slow, torturous circles. "I want to go home with your scent on me. Cum on my face, sweetheart." He flicked fiercely at the little nub before sucking it into his mouth, taking long pulls like he was nursing from a bottle of sweet wine. Fire burned through my body as release pummeled through my system and sent a tidal wave of sensations crashing through every single nerve. My thighs shook beneath his hands, and my toes curled behind his back. Shallow, satiated breaths beat up my chest like I was desperate for oxygen. Something about Beau stole all the air from my lungs and left me needy and desperate for more of his particular brand of sweet torment.

"Look how pretty you are after you cum." His thready voice brought me back to reality, and his lips pressed against mine, his tongue thrusting into my mouth. I tasted the musky-sweet nectar that glistened on his lips, the dark stubble smattering his jaw covered in my scent just like he'd wanted.

"I've never done that before. I've never been with a man," I whispered softly, the words tumbling out before I could stop them.

Beau's eyes softened, and he kissed me slowly, his hands in my hair, his lips taking their time, his tongue tracing the bow and nipping at the corner before he plundered my mouth again. I felt like a decadent dessert he wanted to savor as we kissed for what seemed like hours, losing track of time. I felt the press of his thick erection against my pelvis with every breath, but he never tried for more. He seemed content to please me with his tongue, then kiss me until I was blue in the face.

It was magical.

FOUR

Beau

I'd walked her back to the house, my palm pressed at her back, thinking for the first time in more than thirty years, I was taken away by a woman. If you'd asked me a month ago if I thought soul mates, true love, and fate were a thing I would have said *hell no*, but after meeting my *petite rouge*, I'd argue the point with any man. Love at first sight was real, and Scarlet had socked me in the balls with it.

She'd fallen into my arms and stolen every beat of my heart. I didn't understand it, and I'd tried to fight the feelings raging through my system, tried everything in my power. But it's taken barely any time with the sassy little redhead in my life to realize I was powerless to fight. My mind was obsessed with her, my body even more so. I wondered if she was settling in okay, if Ms. Fair was treating her well, where she'd come from and even what her parents were like. I wanted to claim Scarlet Fair for myself, but I wanted to know her, too. And I was sure that electrical charge that pulsed through my blood whenever she was nearby wasn't felt by me alone. I saw the way her eyes sparkled with interest when I spoke.

I wasn't a man who minced words, I wore my heart on my sleeve and didn't do well with secrets and games. What would she think if I told her exactly what I was feeling about her? That her wild, fiery hair haunted me at night, her effortless giggle and high-beam smile through the day. I couldn't get her off my mind.

Tonight we'd crossed a line, and I couldn't bring

25

myself to regret it. I wanted her so badly I could taste the desire in my mouth. I had a burning desire to take care of her, dote on her, protect her from the big, bad world. I'd throw myself in front of a truck to save her life, drop to my knees and beg for her love and attention. I didn't know what would happen if she didn't feel the same way, didn't want the same things. I would sacrifice everything to have her in my arms, and my heart would split in half if she decided I wasn't the man for her.

I walked down the path bordering the woods to where my little cabin was tucked away. More than a half mile from the main house, I sucked in great lungfuls of air and swore I could still smell her on me. The sweet scent of her pussy clinging to the course whiskers of my beard made my pulse pound painfully through my cock. I slid my hand across my face, relishing the scent of her on me. I was as good as claimed by Scarlet as she was by me.

My heart swelled with protective pride when she'd told me she was a virgin. I was the only one to lay hands on her, the only one to know her taste and the feel of her pressed against my lips, and I damn sure planned on keeping it that way. Owning her with my tongue and my fingers, I'd barely been able to control myself from taking her, but my only concern was doing it right for her. Every woman deserved to be loved and cherished, and tonight I made it my own personal mission to serve her, in my bed and out.

I shook my head and stomped up the steps of my cabin, headed for the kitchen and grabbing a beer before settling on the front porch. My eyes looked out over the horizon, down the pathway I'd just come, past the cherry orchards and the big house in the distance beyond.

I knew for a fact Scarlet couldn't see my little home tucked into the woods, but I was suddenly very glad I had a view of her window. My beautiful *petite rouge*. She deserved someone who would give her the moon and be willing to go all the way there and back to take care of her, and I would damn well make sure I was going to be that man.

Early the next morning I woke with a raging hard-on and a memory of Scarlet so powerful I swore she was in bed with me. I pulled myself from the sheets and walked across the dark wooden floors to the master bathroom. Catching a glance of myself in the mirror, I tried to see myself through Scarlet's eyes. Broad, trim physique, sun-kissed skin from years of outdoor work, a slightly unkempt beard, and short dark hair in contrast to golden flesh. I ran a hand through my hair as I wondered if I should go to her today. I needed to make sure she was okay, that we were okay after everything that had happened last night.

I jumped under the hot spray of the shower as thoughts of my sweet Scarlet swallowed my time. I scrubbed shampoo through my hair, enjoying the feel of the hot water lashing my skin, before I rinsed and wrapped a towel around my waist. I was headed for the kitchen when I spotted a vision walking down my narrow driveway.

"Scarlet?" I swung open my front door and called.

Her gaze darted up, the sun casting a halo of light around her thick red hair. "Oh! I didn't know you lived here. I was just out for a walk." She paused and tilted her palms together.

A smile pulled at my lips. "Well, ya found me." I

sauntered down the steps and snagged her elbow. "Good morning."

I pulled her to me, our bodies bumping together just close enough to heighten the static energy already vibrating between us. "Shoulda brought you home with me last night." I placed a kiss on her nose. "Christ, I missed you."

Scarlet's eyes widened for a breath before she pulled away and touched the pad of her thumb to the bow of her lips. "You missed me?"

My grin turned deeper as I locked her hand in mine, pulling her against my body. "'Course I did. Were you thinkin' about me, too?" A cocky grin stretched my face. "You were, weren't you, *petite rouge*?" I ran a palm up her thigh. Her pretty lips parted and she responded.

"I couldn't stop thinking about you."

"That's a girl. I like being on your mind." My hands cupped the curvy swell of her beautiful ass. "I like knowing I obsess you as much as you do me."

Her eyes widened with my words.

"I can feel your heartbeat, little one." I placed a flat palm over her chest and savored the physical reactions I wrung from her body. "Do I scare you?"

Scarlet's eyes darted up at my words, then she glanced down at her hands again. "Yes," she said with some bravado, before her eyes softened and the smallest of smiles twitched at her lips. "But you excite me, too."

I nearly lost my mind at her small admission. "Aw, Scarlet. You do so much more than excite me." My eyes traced the petite features of her face before landing on her lips. "I've never met anyone quite like you."

"What does that mean?" she laughed sweetly.

"It means I can't stop thinking about you. Everything

about you possesses my mind until the only thing I see is you, the only thing I think about is you, the only thing I dream about," I paused to run a lock of her hair through my fingers, "is you."

"Beau," she breathed, and I pressed my lips against hers in a demanding kiss.

"You're mine, *petite rouge*, and I'll spend every day of the rest of my life proving it to you."

"Yours?" Scarlet's eyes burned with supercharged emotion.

"Think I'd taste you like I did last night and not call you mine?" I wrapped one hand around her neck and pulled her to me, taking her in a kiss and thrusting my aching cock against her pelvis. "If my words aren't enough, I'm happy to show you just how *mine* you are." I held her face in my palm and delved past her lips again.

Her slow, languid kisses consumed me as I gave myself over to her. She could have everything, everything I'd ever worked for, my home, my life. I'd lay it at her feet if she promised to let me in.

"I put my tongue on you. You're mine just as much as if you wore my brand." I murmured at the shell of her ear. A slow shiver crawled down her neck, her elegant throat working for a moment before she replied.

"Beau, I really just came here for a walk. I swear I wasn't looking for you or chasing you after last night or something weird like that." Her words came out in a cute little ramble.

"Sure, Scarlet," I teased and pulled her knuckles to mine for a reverent kiss. "I've got to get to the greenhouse 'fore the guys give me shit." I shoved my nose deep into her hair, taking my fill of her lavender scent before I had to release her. "I'll come for you later."

"Later?" Her eyes shone with excitement. "Okay, I can't wait." She pressed up on her toes to reach my lips, her feather-light kiss nearly bursting my heart with happiness.

"Christ." I pulled her forehead to mine and kissed and nibbled at her lips. "What are you doing to me?"

Her soft laugh fell in the wind. "You said that already."

"I mean it more every time. I'm not sure if you're the best thing for me or the worst, but damned if I can't help but find out."

She shook her head with a laugh before letting go of my hand and backing down the driveway. "Have a good day at work, *Mr. Loup!*"

I almost chased her down like a dog and punished her for her *Mr. Loup* taunt. Instead, I shook my head, a cheesy grin pulling at my cheeks as I adjusted my cock while I watched her go, the outline of her shapely little body in the thin fabric not leaving much to my overactive imagination.

"Change that dress!" I called after her.

She giggled, and I knew her face had turned that bright shade of pink.

Scarlet Fair may very well be the death of me.

FIVE

Scarlet

Beau dropped by Gran's house later that afternoon to update her on the progress of the greenhouse. I'd bitten my lip and listened patiently as they spoke, enjoying the stretch and pull of his muscles as he gestured and explained things to her. He was rough around the edges, all man, incredibly intimidating with his wide stance and crossed arms, but the warmth in his dark eyes drew me in. The cut of his jaw hidden beneath that dark beard haunted the backs of my eyelids. The memory of his sandpaper fingertips tracing across my body was so distracting I thought about excusing myself.

After speaking, Gran offered Beau a slice of the cherry pie, freshly baked by her personal chef. The crimson fruit oozed out of the flaky crust, and I'd taken slow bites, my eyes trained on the soft dip of Beau's lips as he'd smiled brightly and chatted, exchanging friendly pleasantries with her as he ate the confection.

But I caught his looks out of the corner of my eye. I caught the wolfish gaze that cut across the table when I'd leaned over to take a bite. The way he'd swallowed as I chewed. The way my body tingled and ached at the memory of his touch, imagining his lips covering me in cherry-scented kisses.

When Beau finally stood to leave, my body was ablaze with need.

I placed a kiss on Gran's soft cheek as she got up, ready to retire to her room.

31

She'd patted me on the arm, "Such a sweet girl, my Scarlet." And tears had hovered at the edges of her eyelids. "Isn't she the sweetest thing on the planet, Beau?" Gran cooed, an innocent smile darting from Beau to me. My cheeks flushed instantly as Beau stepped up.

"She's sweet indeed." His low voice melted through my veins.

"Goodnight, Beau." Gran placed a kiss on his bearded cheek before climbing the stairs.

"Give me thirty minutes and I'll come for you," Beau whispered at my earlobe and sent a delicious shiver coursing through me.

"Okay," I responded, hardly able to hear my own thoughts over the pounding in my ears.

"I thought I told you to change this dress," he growled and slipped a finger through the flimsy strap. Gran had only just left. What if she turned around? What if she caught us? I quickly backed away, thoughts of my gran catching us raging in my mind.

"Is something wrong with my dress?" I purred.

Beau's eyes narrowed as he assessed me, his eyes finally flashing in warning. "You know exactly what's wrong with it. Makes every damn man on this property look at you when you walk by. Is that what you want? Every man's eyes on you?" He leaned in, pressing me against the wall. "Or just mine?"

My lungs nearly collapsed when his hands came to my waist, his lips trailing across the hollow of my throat. I couldn't breathe. He was stealing my oxygen, stealing my sense.

"Your eyes only." A soft hiss escaped my mouth when his lips attacked my throat, and he laved wet kisses across my skin.

"Thirty minutes," he growled as his hand clutched at the soft flesh of my bottom. "Be ready for me."

"Should I change?" I whimpered, wishing desperately he wouldn't leave so soon.

"No use now." His eyes gleamed with promise. "Anyway, I want to peel it off you with my teeth."

Beau turned and exited through the main door, leaving me weak-kneed and flustered, missing his presence and desperate for his touch again. How could he turn me to silly putty with just a few words?

After running a brush through my hair and adding a shine of lip gloss in the mirror, I found myself fidgeting and waiting at the edge of the patio.

I didn't know what I was doing or what I was thinking, but I knew I trusted Beau, and I also knew I wanted him like nothing I'd ever wanted in my life.

I finally leaped down the few steps, walking confidently towards the orchard. I couldn't wait anymore. At the very least I could wander through the trees and waste some time as I walked to his cabin. Maybe I would run into him on the way.

I wandered down the dark path until I reached the cherry trees, turning down a long row and stretching my fingers out to dust across the shiny skins of the hanging fruit.

I sucked in a deep breath, reveling in the sweet scent that clung to the night air. I took a sharp turn down another row, slowly wandering toward the back of the property and Beau.

A few birds sang in the treetops as the warm summer breeze dusted across my kneecaps, tickling the hem of the summer dress that fell at my thighs. Beau had every right to be upset with me for wearing this dress. It was a tad too small, and I hadn't even realized it when I'd packed it, but my curves had filled out in the few months over the winter since I'd last worn it.

My cleavage was more generous, the heavy flesh of my breasts stretching the neckline.

And he was right on another count. I'd worn it for him. All him. He saw through me easily, and somehow that brought me comfort. Although it'd been such a short time, it felt like he knew me, inside and out, like we were the same somehow. It was inexplicable and thrilling and a little bit scary. He was so hard to my soft, so rough to my gentle, and every wild piece of him thrilled me to the core.

I refocused my attention to the present as I picked my way through the heavy fruit trees, fingertips sending the glossy globes dancing as I passed, before I stepped out onto the main path and straight into a familiar wall of a chest.

"Wandering late at night isn't your best decision, *petite rouge*. I told you I would come for you." Beau's grip tightened at my elbows as he hauled me against his body.

I sucked in a long, slow breath, enjoying the heavy scent of leather and wood compliments of his natural scent and soap, which were purely intoxicating. "I was anxious to see you."

"I see that." His hands were roaming across my body, as if he was as desperate as I was for physical connection. "But next time listen to me. Never know what big bad wolf you may run into." Beau dipped his head and sucked at the flesh of my neck.

"What happens," Beau presented me with a freshly

picked cherry between his fingers, "if I kidnap you, *petite rouge*?" He dipped the cherry across the hot skin of my chest as he spoke, my heart dancing along with the dip and bob of the cherry. "Steal you back to my house and bury myself between your sweet thighs again?" My heart hammered as he lowered the cherry into the dip of my cleavage, secreting it in the flesh between my breasts. The skin of the fruit was cool against the flame of my aroused body.

"Mm, matches the flush on your cheeks." Beau pulled the cherry from between my breasts and popped it into his mouth, his teeth piercing the delicate fruit, his gaze piercing my heart. He whipped the stem with core behind him and lifted me into his arms, my ankles locking around his waist as our lips joined. My hands delved into his hair as our tongues forged together, as if we'd been starved for a taste.

This was beautiful, this was euphoria, this was paradise on earth, colliding together in a violent, primal symphony.

His heavy grunts echoed in the night air around us, before he dropped me to the ground, his fingers locking with mine as he carried us on long strides towards his cabin.

"Wait! My shoe," I blundered, hopping as I bent to slip the heel strap back on my foot.

"Fuck the shoes." Before I could think, he'd launched me over his shoulder, one shoe in hand, the other large palm striped across my barely covered bottom. "Everything about you teases me, draws me in, like bees to a flower I want your nectar. I need the taste of you on my tongue, or I might die of thirst. There's nothing between us tonight, sweet Scarlet.

We reached the steps of his porch, and he walked in, carrying me across the threshold like a caveman.

"Listen, *petite rouge*." He set me on my feet and pressed me against a wall, hands in my hair, eyes boring into me. "I take you to my bed, you're mine. That's it. You don't fight it. I keep you, I take care of you, you'll never have to lift a finger again, but consider yourself owned." His words overwhelmed me, his fierce kiss consumed me, and without even thinking, I nodded.

"I don't share. That means no more dresses that show men these pretty tits." His hands pulled down the neckline of my dress, and he grabbed the flesh in generous fistfuls. "Because they're mine." His tongue found my pert nipple, and he took it between his lips in long, slow sucks, his vibrant eyes trained on mine the whole time.

The intimacy was powerful. I moaned and shifted on my feet, thinking I might fall right onto his floor it felt so good.

"You taste better than I remembered." Beau turned his attention to my other nipple while his hand spread my thighs, one thumb sliding beneath the damp fabric of my panties and gliding through my sex. I arched on my tiptoes, every nerve in my body feeling coiled tight like a spring.

"I didn't think I'd ever find anyone like you," he murmured. His teeth caught the fabric of my dress, and he pulled it down my body, over my hips, until it pooled on the floor, leaving me in nothing but a pair of pure white cotton panties.

His eyes flicked up and down my body, his hands at my hips, then pulled me against him, his nose nestling at the mound at my thighs, sucking in a long inhale.

"This sweet, delicious pussy is mine forever, hear me, Scarlet?" He pushed a finger inside my body.

"Yes, Beau." I sighed, one hand on his shoulder to support myself as he pushed my panties aside and attacked my slit with his deft tongue. He flicked in quick laps, his finger working inside my body, massaging at a spot deep inside that had lust addling my brain.

Arousal and sensation pumped through my bloodstream, and he hoisted my thighs across his shoulders, pressing me against the wall of his cabin and fucking me with his tongue until stars shot across my vision. My eyelids fell, and I succumbed to the pleasure he gave. He added another finger, his tongue drawing on the sensitive bud in long sucks, his thumb swirling at my back entrance and leaving my body feeling completely overwhelmed in a thousand delicious ways.

"Taking this sweet body in every way, Scarlet. I'm owning every single inch of it with my tongue. I'll show you pleasure you didn't even know existed. I've been waiting so long for you," he murmured against me before sliding me down his body, caressing my skin with every hard inch of him. "I haven't been with anyone in so long. It's been years, Scarlet. And even then, I was always safe. I always used a condom." He paused to place a gentle kiss on my lips. "But there's no protection needed between us. You and I are forever, and I want you bare. I need to feel every last raw nerve of you. I need to know how I make you feel." He kissed me slowly as his forehead pressed against mine.

His words left me reeling. He hadn't been with anyone in years? Why me? Why now? There was nothing about me that was that special. I was always invisible to men. I blended into the background. They always wanted the sexy girls, not the quiet, shy ones. Now, here with Beau, I felt powerful. He made me feel special. He made me blossom. Being with Beau, feeling his touch, was like being jolted back to life. He was a magnet, and every part of me was attracted to him and in desperate need for more.

"Tell me I can have all of you." He placed a palm over my thundering heart. I stopped, my eyes trained on his, and saw the burning flames in his eyes. This strong, virile man wanted me. He wanted every single part of me, leaving me powerless to resist.

"Yes, Beau. Yes, I want to feel you. I want to feel everything." I wrapped my hands around his neck and pulled him to me for a long kiss. I heard his grunts, felt the press of his pleasure between us in the form of his rock-hard erection. I wanted to show him what he meant to me. I wanted to give him something back. "Let me make you feel good," I stammered and dropped to my knees, my palms trailing the roughly etched carvings of his abdominal muscles.

"Mm, *petite rouge*." One of his arms pushed into the threads of my hair, holding my head gently as I worked at the buttons on his pants. Pulling the zipper down, the fabric fell loose around his hips, the deep cut of his pelvic muscles and that sexy V I'd only seen on the men in magazines made my mouth water.

"I want to see those pretty lips around my cock." He caressed my cheek, the contrast between the gentle touch and his coarse words turning me on even more.

I grasped the waistband of his pants and boxers and pulled them down his toned hips, his heavy erection springing out, aimed directly at me. My heart thundered as I thought about what it would feel like buried inside my body.

"You're so big." I swallowed the lump in my throat as I gripped the hot flesh in my small fist.

His soft chuckle filled the air. "Better to please you with." His thumb traced my lips as he spoke, the tip of his dick leaking pre-cum just inches from my mouth.

I sucked him past my lips, hollowing my cheeks as best I could, only hoping it felt good for him.

"Suck it up, sweetheart," he crooned, and instantly, as if he were my favorite ice-cream flavor, I trailed the length of his dick with my tongue before sucking the tip back into my mouth. Beau's eyes rolled back in his head, encouraging me to continue. I sucked down the length of his shaft again, this time taking him deeper than I had before and tasted the salty drops of his pre-cum at the back of my tongue.

"Mm, this mouth was made for me." He pulled me from the floor before I could finish, his lips attaching instantly to mine as our tongues tangled in a feral coupling. His hands tore at my body, leaving his mark on every inch of me, his scent washing my skin and claiming me as thoroughly as if I wore his ring.

Beau had truly captured me, body and soul.

SIX

Beau

I hoisted my beautiful girl in my arms and carried her down the hallway like it was our wedding night. I wished it would have been, she meant that much to me. She meant everything, and I had every intention of not just telling her, but showing her how much.

I considered myself a man who read people well. I talked less and listened often, and something in her eyes had told me she was made for me and me alone. Something had sparked between us from the very first moment, and it had all been leading up to this moment. I only hoped she knew what I meant when I said I owned her. I didn't do half-ass.

I'd gone through a lifetime of hurt, and I'd always known that when I found the woman for me, I would feel it churning through my veins like a magic elixir, exactly how Scarlet made me feel.

Did I want to bend her will and convince her to stay with me forever? Hell yes! Would I? With everything in my power, but only as long as I saw that smile dance across her cheeks, heard that laugh bubble up from her belly, watched that flirty flip of her hair that let me know that she felt it too. My only concern was for her: her happiness, her health, her heart. Mostly her heart. I wanted to burrow myself deep inside it, she wouldn't even know I was there until she didn't remember life without me. She'd already found her way into mine.

"Scarlet," I growled as I pushed my way through the master bedroom, hearing the door crash against the wall as I laid her down on the large king bed.

"Will it hurt?" Her fingers danced across my shoulders, driving me mad with desire.

I took her lips in a gentle kiss, my hands caressing her body like I was fashioning a delicately crafted piece of art. "I'm afraid so, baby. I'm sorry."

"Promise to go slow?" Her fear nearly punctured my heart, and I wished with everything I had that I could skip this painful part for her.

"Hey." I took her face in my hands, gazed into her eyes, and saw every single dream for my future. "You don't have to ask me that. I would never do anything to hurt you. I will always do everything it takes to stop you from feeling pain. I promise I'll go slow. I promise if it gets to be too much, I'll stop. And most of all, I promise to kiss away any pain you may have until all you remember is the good parts."

I hooked the elastic of her underwear in my palm and pulled them down her legs. "I promise to always take care of you, anytime, day or night. Call my name and I'll be there." I placed a kiss at the soft swell of her hip. "We're connected, you and me. I can feel you here." I covered my heart with her palm in mine. "When you hurt, when you cry, when you worry, I feel it. We're the same person, Scarlet. Our flames were split long ago, we just had to find each other again." I nuzzled against her ear. "I've been looking for you."

Scarlet smiled deeply, overwhelming emotion radiating in her eyes as she gazed up at me. "Well, what took you so long?"

"Been right here all along, baby." A rakish grin crossed my face, as I crawled up her body and cupped her cheeks in my palms. "From this moment forward, I'm always right here."

Her sweet eyes welled with tears before a slow smile curved her rosy lips. "Thank you," she whispered and pulled my head down, kissing me, her tongue pushing past my lips to dance with mine. I thrust my hips against her, my desperate cock anxious to be buried so far inside her I could forget every painful thing that had ever happened to me before her.

"I'm ready, Beau. I want to feel you." Her seraph voice nearly tore my heart up.

"You're my everything, Scarlet. I just want you to know that." I placed a kiss on her lips again, easing my erection between her thighs, feeling it make contact with the hot, wet flesh of her beautiful pussy for the first time.

I sucked in a sharp breath, feeling overwhelmed as I got ready to enter her.

Take it slow. Be the man she deserves.

"I'm going slow, baby." I kissed across her jaw as I pressed the tip of my dick between her hot lips. Her body arched, and her legs wrapped around my waist, grinding her hot little core against my dick and nearly making me lose my ever-loving mind.

"No, don't do that." I rested my forehead against hers, my muscles strung tight as I tried to control my breaths. "I'll never be able to take it slow if you keep grinding against me like that."

Her soft chuckle surprised me and sent Cupid's blazing arrow straight to my heart. "I want to feel you, Beau. I want you inside me." Her voice lowered one sexy octave as her hand ran across my back.

"Mm." I slid my dick between her silky lips, massaging her clit with the tip, trying to lubricate her as best I could to prevent the pain I knew was coming. "So glad I found you, *petite rouge*."

SEVEN

Scarlet

I sucked in one lungful of air after another as I felt the slow stretch of Beau's cock filling my body. A thousand angry needles pinched at the sensitive flesh, my nerves protesting as my muscles locked and tried to prevent him from plunging himself further. He was too big, way too big, much larger than average, I assumed.

"Shh, baby, just relax, deep breaths and let your body adjust to me." His words soothed me as his hands worked apart the flesh of my thighs. I sucked in as I felt the relaxation of my muscles, the slow burn fading to a slight pinch before my breathing turned to normal and I loosened my legs.

"That's my girl." His hands were in my hair, his lips kissing across my cheeks and jaw. "That's my beautiful girl." He pushed in again, millimeter by millimeter, and I found his invading flesh didn't hurt me like it first had. My body relaxed, the pain turning to a soft throb, before nearly melting away completely. Beau's thumb slid between our bodies, his digit swirling at the engorged flesh as my pants began to pick up for a totally different reason.

"Slow, baby, we're going slow," he murmured, as my hips began an anxious rocking of their own. Beau's palm tightened at my hip as he tried to still me, but I was too far gone. This felt so good. Suddenly it felt like he was touching the most intimate parts of me, and it was thrilling, all-consuming, so many sensations overwhelming every system of my body.

"Beau, I want to feel you…deeper," I begged, and his nostrils flared, his eyes raking up and down my body beneath him before his hands plumped at the flesh of my breasts, one thumb and finger pinching at the cool bud before releasing it again.

"Drew me in from the start. No wonder I couldn't stop thinking of you, *petite rouge*." Beau placed a decadent kiss on my lips as he slid his cock deeper inside me. I arched and groaned, my fingernails digging into his skin as I breathed through the slice of pain shooting from the inside out. "Such a little firecracker."

"You're so big, I didn't think it would feel this good," I gasped as a slow orgasm built in my body, the base of my spine burning with an overwhelming sensation.

"I knew it would be this way. I tried to fight it, tried to fight you, tried to fight my feelings, but damn if you didn't steal every breath in my body. I've lived a long time without you, Scarlet. Not gonna live a day longer."

He pinched at the precious little bud he'd been working, and my release burned through my body, eating up all the energy in my muscles and sending me jetting into another galaxy. Nothing existed beyond his arms around me, the feel of him buried so far inside me, the soft touch of his lips, the rough pads of his thumbs. His scent curled around my nostrils, and I was lost, surrounded by him in every sense of the word.

"Never letting you go," Beau gritted as his body shuddered, his hands clenching at my thighs, as he yanked his erection from my body, long hot jets of his semen splashing across my stomach. I watched fascinated as he milked the flesh of his erection, sweet agony covering his tortured face. The clench of his jaw and the furrow of his brow as he released himself on me was the most gorgeous thing I'd ever seen.

I licked my lips, desperate to have him all over again. Desperate to feel him cum deep inside me, coat me and claim me from the inside out.

"Love you smelling like me." Beau began to rub the white semen across my body, over my breasts, across my navel, around my mound, and dipping his long middle finger inside my soaked core. "Consider that my brand, baby. Just try wearing that dress again and see what happens." His cocky grin sent a wave of surprise crashing through me as his words curled my stomach, making me want to burrow into his arms. He said all the right things, and I loved every minute of it.

He tucked me under his large arm, and I curled myself around him, drowsy with sex and lust.

"Next time I'm gonna cum inside you."

I couldn't help the giggle that escaped my mouth. I leaned over and pressed a flirty kiss on his lips. "I can't wait."

"Mm…damn, *petite rouge*. If you only knew what you did to me."

EIGHT

Beau

I woke early the next morning, excitement coiling my gut and tightening my dick. Scarlet had slept in my arms, in my bed all night. The thought made me almost giddy. In so many ways Scarlet was my first, and she would be my last. She was it for me.

I couldn't breathe for a single damn moment without her. I couldn't fathom a life without her sparkling eyes and the tinkling laugh that sent long-dormant butterflies sputtering in my gut.

I grinned, hearing the soft breath of her next to me. I rolled over, trying not to wake her. The creamy white sheet fell over the swell of her breast, one graceful arm bent at the elbow as she slept, her lips parted and her hair a wild fucking mess of waves on the pillow around both of us.

She was a goddamn angel, and I was a slave to her love.

I traced a fingertip across the pillowy flesh of her breast, pulling the sheet down just a fraction and watching as her succulent nipple budded in the cool morning air. I grinned, my thumb darting across the peaked flesh as my mouth began to water and my dick began a slow throb. I'd need to have her this morning, and every morning. I loved my scent on her skin, warning every other asshole off, but even more than that

I wanted to empty myself inside her. Claim her as mine, put my baby deep inside her sweet body and keep her in my home and in my bed forever.

I'd raise ten babies with her and be the happiest man on earth. Her nurturing warmth and stubborn spark reminded me of my own sweet mother, and I knew instantly that Scarlet had burrowed her way into my heart much more than I'd even realized.

I pushed a hand through my hair, determined to let her sleep a while longer and thinking I could make her something for breakfast before I left for work this morning, so I stumbled into the kitchen naked. I hadn't been this happy in too long, probably forever.

I poured a glass of orange juice before gazing out the window. My eyes landed on the rows of cherry trees in the distance, the immaculately landscaped gardens of the main house, and the small groves of evergreens sheltering the stately manor.

It was a beautiful home, that's for sure, but I was perfectly happy right where I was. I'd renovated this cabin with my own two hands. I had a thriving business and the ability to do just about anything my heart desired, but the one thing I wanted more than anything may prove to be the hardest to attain.

Her.

I wasn't a foolish man. I understood the world was tough, and a man like me didn't marry a girl like her. Seeing that house, I wouldn't be surprised if she came from a world of private schools and parties. I was a simple man, and working with my hands under the hot rays of the sun was one of my greatest joys. It was a life I preferred, but not one that many understood.

"Morning," a voice sweeter than any angel I could

fathom carried across my kitchen. I turned to find her wrapped in one of my plaid shirts, not a thing else.

"Scarlet." My cock flexed and throbbed as I closed the distance between us. "Fuck, you're beautiful in my shirt." I cupped her neck and slid my tongue between her lips, enjoying the taste of her on my tongue. "Thank you for spending the night with me." I placed a slow, languid kiss on her mouth.

"Thank you for giving me such a wonderful night." Her grin crooked to one side and caused my dick to twitch.

I weaved my palms beneath the shirt she wore and made contact with her hot flesh. "We'd better get moving before I lose myself inside you again."

"Mm, sounds like the perfect start to the day," her pouty lips murmured against mine.

"Tempting." I kissed her lips again. "Very tempting. You're welcome to stay here. I'd love nothing more than to come home to you, barefoot on the front porch, greeting me wearing nothing but a smile, but I think I heard something about reading to Gran this mornin', and I don't want you to miss that."

I cupped her ass in my palms and pulled her lower half against me, my morning erection pressed against her body and begging to sink inside her. My instinct was to have a chat with Ms. Fair and tell her Scarlet was mine and that she would be staying with me at my place for the rest of the summer, no two ways about it, but I recognized the situation was delicate. I couldn't exactly beat my chest and haul her over my shoulder and steal her away, no matter how much I secretly wanted to.

"Think she'll be okay that you stayed out all night?"

"Oh, I dunno." She furrowed her brow. "She's usually

not awake and around till later, so she may not even notice, but I'm eighteen, so it shouldn't be an issue anyway, right?"

"I hope not." I kneaded at her shoulders. "Now let's get in the shower. I want to get my soapy hands all over you."

Scarlet laughed before turning, a soft breeze catching the hem of my shirt and revealing the delicious curve of her ass cheek.

"Fuck, you wear these things around me on purpose." I slapped at her cheek playfully. "You could use a punishment for all the teasing you've been doing." I caught her by the waist and nipped at her earlobe as we stepped into my master bathroom.

"I don't know what you're talking about, Mr. Loup." Scarlet turned, landing a cocky grin of her own on me.

"Pretty little liar." I grinned and caught her chin, holding it in place as I kissed her deeply, plunging my tongue past her lips and down her throat. "I want this ass so bad I won't be able to think straight at work today. You're dangerous for a man like me, *petite rouge*."

"Why?" She spun, one of her arms suddenly around my neck, her leg hitched around my thigh.

"You make me want things I'm afraid you're not ready to give." I hoisted her onto the bathroom counter, thrusting my cock between her legs and pushed the plaid fabric down her shoulders, using the arms to tie her wrists behind her back. "Look at those pretty tits thrust out for me." I held the weight of one in my hand, pinching her nipple a moment before moving on to the other. "You like when I look at you like this?"

She nodded her head, her chest heaving in labored, lust-filled pants.

"I wasn't going to take you this morning." I pushed her thighs apart and settled myself between them, sliding my dick in her silky hot slit and holding on to the few thin threads of control I had left. "And I'm still not, but clearly you want my attention." My fingertips danced across her heavy breasts. "And mark my words, I own all your pleasure. The day you leave this house unsatisfied is the day I fail as your lover."

"L-lover?" Her eyes flickered open and closed again.

"Bet your sweet ass I'm your lover. Didn't I make it clear last night?" I grinned, catching her bottom lip between my teeth as she rocked her hips fiercely against my cock.

"Yes." She shuddered as I felt her pulse and shake around me.

"So sensitive." I swirled her arousal on my fingertips and trailed it up her skin, painting the glistening path across one nipple before landing at the bow of her lips. I pushed my finger into her mouth. "See what I do to you?" I husked as I watched her tongue whirl across my digit, tasting the arousal coating my finger. Her eyes lowered with lust as she sucked and pulled, cleaning my finger like she was starved for the taste.

"Now get in the shower. I've got to get to work, and you've got to spend some time with Gran." I pulled her from the counter and landed another swift smack on her ass. "This is mine tonight." I rubbed at the flesh of her ass cheek, then landed another swift smack, watching her milky flesh pink up nicely.

"Beau!" Scarlet turned after the second smack, her eyes wide as she rubbed at her cheek, a beautiful blush creeping up her chest.

"My mark on your skin looks good," I said, the only

thing going through my head at that moment. "Now get in the shower before I do it again."

NINE

Scarlet

"Christ, woman, you can't wear that. I thought we talked about this." Beau's large body covered the distance between us in a heartbeat, his fingers pulling at the torn strap that had once helped hold my dress on.

"I don't have anything else, and someone got a little wild last night." I gestured to the hem, a new slit up the side seam that revealed more thigh that it had last night.

"Shit." Beau thrust a hand through his hair, then rummaged through some drawers and pulled out a soft, blue, plaid shirt. "Put this on over it at least."

"You're being silly," I giggled, but secretly enjoyed his doting hands pulling the warm cotton up my arms and over my shoulders. I sniffed the cool soapy scent of his laundry soap and let my eyes flutter closed for just a second.

"Damn, you look even more beautiful now." He caught my chin between his fingers and pulled me in for a soft kiss. My hands wrapped around his neck on instinct, my mouth open and welcoming him as I melted against his body.

A low rumble fell from his lips as he broke the kiss and held me at arm's length. "Wish like hell I didn't have to work today."

"It's okay. I have a hundred things to do." I buttoned the shirt around my torn dress as I spoke.

"Well, make it a hundred and one. I want you back

here with me tonight." Beau pulled a pair of jeans up his strong legs and pulled a clean white shirt from his drawer.

"Yes, Mr. Loup." A Cheshire cat grin turned my lips.

His growl was the only response I got before his hands were at my waist and he was spinning me in his arms. As he bent me over the bed, he pulled up his crisp shirt and the hem of my dress, his palm stroking my bare bottom as if he adored it. I missed its absence a moment later when he landed a swift spank on my right cheek.

"Ow!" I jumped and squirmed, his palm pressed at my back, preventing me from getting far.

"Mm, love seeing my handprint on your ass, *petite rouge*." He stroked the fading sting with his palms, leaving me surprisingly comforted. "Now, say thank you."

Lust rocketed through my brain. Thank you? He expected me to thank him after a spanking?

"Scarlet?" his delicious tenor sing-songed.

"What if I don't want to?" I turned, taunting but with an undertone of seriousness.

One dark eyebrow rose, and his fingers slipped through my dripping sex, swirling arousal across the skin of my thighs. "Thank me, *petite rouge*."

I watched riveted as he slipped his finger, coated in my juices, into his mouth and sucked it clean.

"Thank you, Beau."

"Mmm…I'm saving the rest of you for tonight." He grinned wickedly and helped me off the bed, righting my dress and locking his hand in mine.

Butterflies battered my rib cage as we walked through his cabin hand in hand. Down the front porch steps, the very same he'd carried me over last night, he escorted me outside and into the bright summer sunshine. My eyes glazed as bliss bombarded my brain. I could see myself here, with him, forever. I could see it. I could feel it in my bones. With him, I knew.

"Be a good girl while I'm at work, baby." His warm gaze heated my skin, his lips descending to meet my own. Every nerve in my body tingled when he slipped his arms around my waist, and I pressed up on my tiptoes to return the kiss. I was definitely too short, he was definitely too tall, but together we were perfect.

"I'll miss you," I confessed when we pulled apart.

"Keep kissing me like that and I won't leave." He pressed another kiss to my lips, one of his hands fidgeting at the hem of my dress, dusting my thighs.

"Later?" I backed away, our hands still locked and stretching between us.

He pulled me back to him swiftly, crushing my body against his and landing another dark kiss across my lips, his tongue pushing further, deeper, longer this time. "Later," he murmured when he finished.

I nodded, taking a few tentative steps backward, our gazes still locked. I waved softly, a shy smile on my lips, while his gaze held mine with unwavering intensity.

My cheeks burned with the smile that lit my face. I ran a hand through my hair, relishing the scent of him. My lips were still a little swollen from his kisses, my vagina felt sore and a little raw, but it only reminded me of where I'd been the night before, *where he'd been*.

My fingertips fell on my lips, and I traced the bow, remembering his body pressed against mine.

It was heaven, and he was heaven, and I couldn't imagine a single thing that could shatter this bubble.

TEN

Beau

I smoothed the grout on a row of outdoor tile just as my cell vibrated in my pocket. I had employees who did the manual labor, but I loved the feeling of accomplishment after a hard day's work. There was just something rewarding about hard labor.

"Yeah?" I listened a few moments before my heart slammed to a dead stop.

Emergency. Next of kin. Signatures needed. The words tumbled violently in my head.

"I'll be there as quick as I can." I uttered, hitting end call on the phone before dropping my tools and heading for my truck.

The last goddamn thing I wanted to do was leave right now, but I couldn't live with myself if I stayed. My only priority was getting to the main house to tell Scarlet I had to leave. I wished like hell I could bring her with me, but I knew this was something I'd have to do on my own. The idea of leaving her now felt beyond unbearable, but what kind of man would I be if I did nothing and stayed? She deserved a good man and for her, I wanted to be the best in every way imaginable.

I barreled down the road to the main house, catching sight of Darla as I walked up to the driveway. I gave her a curt nod as I rushed through the front doors, hoping to catch a glimpse of red hair, but settling on Ms. Fair when she turned the corner.

"Have you seen Scarlet?"

"She left for a walk. What's wrong, Beau?" Her

56

worried eyes assessed my near-trembling form.

"I have to go to Pennsylvania."

"Oh no." Her eyes laced with sympathy. She knew. I'd had a weak moment a few weeks ago and confessed to her some of the darkest secrets about my past. I normally didn't open up too easily to people, but Ms. Fair's gentle wisdom and kind heart had made me finally let go.

"I don't want to leave her. She means everything to me, and I want to be good for her, so I have to leave so that I can be worthy of her."

"Beau." She pressed a hand to her mouth as her eyes watered. "Of course. I'll take care of her for you."

"I don't want her to worry, and I know she'll worry about me when I'm gone."

"The only thing you need to worry about is getting on the road."

"Thank you, ma'am. I can't thank you enough." I gently touched her thin arm.

"Be safe, dear. And get back to us soon."

I nodded, relieved the Scarlet would get my message, and someone would take care of my girl.

ELEVEN

Scarlet

"You look gorgeous today, darling. Look at you!" Gran stood and took my hand, spinning me indulgently.

"Having a good day, Gran?" I asked as I took a seat next to her on the wooden swing Beau had made and set up the very first day I was here.

"Wonderful day, the sun is out, what's not to love?"

"It is beautiful, you're very right." I looked up at the bright sun, feeling like its rays were shining just for me. My thoughts trailed back to Beau before I instantly pulled myself back to the present.

"Scarlet, Beau was here earlier. He had to leave unexpectedly."

My ears perked up instantly at the mention of his name. "Leave?"

"He was frantically looking for you. It was when you were out for that walk. He stopped by and said he had a pressing matter in Pennsylvania he had to tend to, but that he would be back as soon as he could." Her eyes twinkled as she relayed the information. "He did sound very concerned about you, I think you've left quite the impression on him."

"Oh, I don't think so, Gran." I tried to wave off her polite concern. I felt the ground under my feet shift. Was I not important enough for him to wait until he could

58

speak to me? What could be so pressing that it couldn't wait another hour? I was foolish to think that he cared. Maybe the time we had spent together wasn't as precious to him as it was to me.

"Please don't think ill of him, it must have been something very important to pull him away. I got the sense that he was not too pleased to be leaving." She winked at me and offered a small smile.

Heat crept up my face. Gran had always been able to read me like a book. She chattered on, and I tuned out, my heart shuddering to a slow stop as I realized I wouldn't see him tonight, maybe not even tomorrow night. I sighed, slumping in my chair and feeling like the day had gone wildly downhill in just the course of a few hours. What could possibly have pulled him away? And why hadn't he waited to tell me before he left?

"Are you ready to read, dear?" The question pulled me from my thoughts.

"Yes, Gran." I smiled brightly and held up the copy of *The Little Prince*, a French classic Gran had requested.

"Good, honey. Now where did we leave off?"

I began to read, my thoughts drifting away to Beau behind the wheel of his truck, driving all day and night to get to whatever had pulled him away in Pennsylvania. And I was here alone. Why hadn't he even tried to tell me? A quick stop before he left? Was it too much to ask? Or was I expecting too much?

He was the only person I'd ever been with, and I didn't want to be one of *those* girls, but deep down I wanted to be one of those girls and scream and beat his chest and tell him I'd just lost my virginity to him last night and now he was gone. The soreness between my legs was the only reminder that it'd even happened at all.

TWELVE

Beau

An old Merle Haggard song pumped through the stereo as miles upon miles of highway stretched before and behind me. Here I was, somewhere over the New York and Pennsylvania state line, and my mind was three hundred miles away on the little saucy redhead who shared my bed last night.

That I'd kissed like the devil had possessed me this morning.

I still hoped she was feeling the sting from my hand on her ass.

It fucking killed me to leave her this morning. But I didn't have another choice. The call had come in just after I'd gotten to the job site.

Emergency. Next of kin. Signatures needed.

The words rattled on repeat in my brain. I should have seen this coming, in some regards I blamed myself for being so far away, but damned if I'd let a mistake like this slip through the cracks again. As soon as I arrived in Pennsylvania, I'd have to walk into that room and take charge, something I didn't like to do, but a position everyone seemed to look to me to fill.

The music filtered through the cab of my truck as I drove, sending my mind back to simpler times before life had taken hold. Everyone chooses their path in life, has their reaction to a hardship, in my case, I'd turned to woodworking, putting everything I had into my business. Age and experience taught me that all too often others turned to a darker side, a coping mechanism to forget the pain instead of dealing with it.

Thank god I'd opened up to Ms. Fair about this very situation a few weeks ago. She'd become a sweet, grandmother-figure for me, an effect she seemed to have on many. Her gentle nature was a balm for my wounded soul. Similar to the effect her granddaughter had on me.

As soon as I returned, I planned on finding Scarlet. I'd knock down the door of the damn mansion if I had to. I was hoping this would be a there and back trip, a day or two at most, but God knows it could be longer. It would all depend on what exactly I was dealing with when I got there.

The sun shone brightly across the evening sky, lighting up the horizon in a blaze of color. My mind fell back on every single moment with Scarlet under my body last night. I knew she probably still felt the pinch this morning, but if anything, she'd seemed more alive. Happier. The rosy cheeks and sparkling eyes nearly blinded me with beauty. She was a vision walking out into my kitchen this morning, and it was my full intention to do everything in my power to keep her there.

A Patsy Cline song filtered across the radio waves, and my heart instantly plummeted. One of my mother's favorites. 'You Belong to Me.'

I remembered her listening to it on repeat and twirling around the kitchen as she sang, the soft threads of her floral dress whispering around her legs. She was like an angel, a dream in my three-year-old perspective. I loved her more than anything, the evenings spent rocking on the porch with a book, the mornings with pancakes and freshly plucked cherries.

I had an idyllic childhood, simple, to be sure, but it was all the carefree happiness a little boy could ask for, until it was all ripped away.

I didn't understand the diagnosis then, but I still remember the chaos at the hospital. I remember the funeral. I remember my dad's tears. I remember my dad crying for days in their bedroom after she was gone. My memories up until the age of three are filled with laughter and love, but every one after is painted with a tar-black brush, until Scarlet.

My father pulled away after that. He was still a good dad. He tried, I knew that. But I think he was too broken to go on without her. He passed when I was only twenty, years of hard work and carrying a broken heart too much for him. I threw myself into my business after he was gone, only going home to collapse in a cold bed at the end of the night. I'd come a long way since then, barely crawling my way out of the darkness intact. Those days made me realize how utterly lonely life is without someone to spend your nights and days with. I'd come to realize life just wasn't worth living if you didn't have someone to laugh with, share the joys and the smiles with. My father's descent into darkness and my own experience with loneliness had taught me that.

I ached to hear Scarlet's voice, feel the velvet threads of her sweet red hair beneath my fingers. I craved her.

THIRTEEN

Scarlet

It'd been two days since I'd seen Beau.

It'd been two days since Gran had heard from him.

"Maybe you should call Beau, make sure everything is okay?" I offered nonchalantly as Gran and I sat, *The Little Prince* and tea spread out between us. I'd fallen asleep with tears hovering in my eyelids, desperate to know how he was, craving his velvet voice and intoxicating touch.

"Oh, I'm sure he's fine, dear. If there was a problem, he would have called." She patted my knee before taking a sip from her porcelain cup. "But what if something did happen to Beau? Who would the police even contact? I think you should call him." I knew I'd crossed the line as soon as I said it.

"Oh? You think so?" Gran's knowing eyes assessed me quickly before returning to her tea cup. "Maybe I'll give him a call this afternoon. Make sure he's all right like you said," she offered, and I knew she was doing it only to appease me.

"Good idea," I mumbled, slumping in my chair, wondering if it would be too much to shake her and demand she call *right now!*

"Chapter six, right?" She picked up the book between us and pressed it into my lap, a sweet smile on her face.

63

I returned the smile and opened the book, starting to read about faraway lands and destiny.

I didn't give two licks for any of it. I wanted to know if Beau was okay. "Everything all right, Scarlet dear?" Gran asked, pulling me from my thoughts and forcing me to focus on the text in front of me.

"Yes, it's just hot out today."

"Well, maybe you should go upstairs and lie down. I heard a truck door out front, so I'm going to wander out there and see if it's Beau."

My eyes widened instantly as my heart galloped out of my chest. How had I missed the sound of a truck door?

"Oh, maybe I'll check with you." I stood, straightening my dress and knowing she saw through my act instantly. She smiled and looped her arm with mine anyway.

"I thought you might want to walk with me, make sure he's okay and all." Her coy smile sent heat radiating up my cheeks.

We walked around the edge of the house, and Beau's black pickup came into view, his broad physique taking long, elegant strides to us.

"Welcome home, Beau!" Gran clasped her hands together, and with more energy in her step than I'd seen all week, she touched his cheek lovingly with an open palm.

My eyes cut to Beau's, our gazes held suspended in the static energy between us.

"You must be parched, let me get you something to drink. Scarlet made some sweet tea this morning..." Gran continued mumbling as she turned back to the house.

"I'll be right back!"

My gaze tore back to his.

If I'd thought for a minute he'd forgotten about me, I was dead wrong.

His intense eyes burned up the space between us, nearly emptying my lungs of all oxygen. Slow, quick pants wracked my body under his heated gaze. I licked my lips and watched as he crossed the distance in long strides, his hand reaching for my elbow instantly.

"Scarlet." He caught my elbow and hauled me against his broad, rigid form. His mouth covered mine, tongue slipping between my lips as his hands roamed my back and bottom. I'd missed him so much it physically hurt.

"Beau," I breathed, a thousand words choking my throat and none of them breaking free.

"Sorry I was gone so long," he said, his lips grazing the shell of my ear when he spoke. "I have to make a few calls, but I want to see you. Come to me tonight."

I only nodded, nearly choking on my own tongue.

"Until later, *petite rouge*?" His rakish grin danced up my body.

I sucked in a breath and croaked, "Later."

"Here we are, dears! A glass for each of us." Gran stepped over the threshold then, a small tray of sweet tea in her hands.

"Gran!" I pulled out of Beau's embrace, hoping she hadn't spied us.

"Let me." Beau took the tray from my grandmother, passing each of us a fancy crystal glass, such a delicate gesture in his rough hands. "It's good to be back." He winked at me and held his glass up in a toast.

My cheeks flamed deeply as the three of us toasted before drinking the sweet amber liquid.

"If you don't mind I've got some things to take care of

before the special reunion I have planned tonight." Beau spoke to Gran, every hair on the back of my neck standing up with his private innuendo.

"We'll have to catch up later, Beau." Gran smiled deeply, and I wondered who was more smitten with him, me or her.

"Will do, ma'am." Beau replied before casting a sidelong glance my way. "Ladies."

He nodded and walked off.

Just like that, he was gone again, leaving me up at this big house alone, my thoughts walking away right along with his sexy gait.

I sighed, feeling drained from just the few minutes of being in his presence, having to pretend there wasn't more between us, when every fiber of my body wanted to run to him.

I turned, heading up to my room for a short nap to calm my nerves and rest before tonight.

Flopping on my bed, I pulled a pillow over my head, trying to calm my racing thoughts and vibrating body before drifting into a restless sleep. Beau Loup enchanted me, like a fly caught in his web, I couldn't escape, and I didn't even want to.

I woke later that evening after the sun had set and dusk was settling in. I shook my head and caught my bearings before I remembered that Beau was home.

It had been too long. I needed to be in his arms, just for a few minutes, just for the reassurance that he was back. I searched the kitchen for something to bring him when my eyes landed on two freshly baked cherry pies. Gran definitely wouldn't mind if I brought one to Beau.

I skipped down the steps and out the patio doors, navy

brushing the landscape in dark shadows. I picked my way down the path to the orchard, then twined my way in and out of the trees on the way to his cabin.

I walked out of the orchard and turned the corner down the driveway to his house, past a small grove of trees, and then the space opened up. I smiled when I saw his truck parked out front.

I sped up when I saw the golden glow of a light on in the kitchen.

I nearly tripped over my own feet when I bounced up the steps to his porch.

I stopped dead in my tracks when I saw Beau, fresh out of the shower and wearing only a pair of low-hanging sweats on his hips.

His eyes locked with mine. "Scarlet?"

FOURTEEN

Beau

Scarlet stood on my porch, a pie held in both hands. I took the pie from her and set it on the table before pulling her into my arms, running my palms down the elegant slope of her back, resting my outstretched hands across her ass as my lips locked with hers in a fevered kiss.

"Thanks for the pie," I murmured between kisses, kicking the door closed and pulling Scarlet into the kitchen with me, pressing her body against the counter and not giving her a single chance to interrupt me. I needed her. Whatever else she may say after this, I needed her fucking lips on mine.

"Beau." She pulled away from me, heavy pants wracking her body.

"Love kissing the breath out of you." I placed another soft kiss on the tip of her nose. "Couldn't get you off my mind while I was gone. Missed the fuck out of you, *petite rouge*."

My palms roamed her skin, lips covering her neck in decadent kisses. "Thank you for waiting for me."

"Of course, I would. Why wouldn't I?"

"I know it was hell… I had to leave. I broke our date." I pressed my forehead against hers. "I had to go save my sister."

"Your sister?" Her eyes widened before understanding

68

settled in.

"She's an addict." I confessed. "She's been on and off the wagon for a few years now. I've tried to help her however I can, but the last time I let her come to my house she stole some of my stuff to pawn." I paused, feeling pain burn in my throat. "She overdosed Monday night. I got the call from a hospital in the town she was living in. She at least had me listed as her emergency contact on her phone. I'm the only person she's got, can you imagine if they wouldn't have been able to find me?"

"Beau...I'm so sorry. I had no idea." She pressed her palms to my cheeks, her touch soothing my anxiety in small increments.

"It's not something I talk about. After my mother died, it was harder and harder on her. It's hard for a little girl to be motherless in the world. My father was starting to decay then. He was a shell of the man he once was. The man who played with us and laughed with such joy slipped away to a lonely man who only received comfort from alcohol. My sister wanted to belong, she longed to be loved. She fell in love with the wrong men and the life of oblivion and escape swallowed her up. Over the years I tried to get her help but one day I couldn't find her anymore--she just disappeared from my life. So when I got the call I had to go. Please tell me you forgive me for running out. I tried to find you, but Gran said you'd gone for a walk. I was desperate to tell you I was leaving, and I'd be back as soon as I could manage it. But I couldn't find you, and I had to get there as fast as I could. I drove ten hours straight to find she was on a heart monitor. Seeing my little sister in that bed," I ran a hand through my hair. "Worst day of my life."

"How is she now?"

"She's in good hands. I brought her to rehab. When I got there, she had been committed to the hospital. I told her I'd pay for ninety days if she'd commit to all of it, they have a facility attached right to the hospital. It's one of the best detox facilities in the country. She's always bailed early. But hopefully, this time it takes."

"Should you go back? Don't stay here for me, Beau. I can wait longer."

"If I go back now it's only if you are with me. I need you, *Petite Rouge*. The only thing that kept me going was getting home to you. I'm no good to her there, sitting around nagging. Besides, she has to be isolated now. They said thirty days without any familial contact." I trailed my palms down the curve of her spine. "I need you so much, Scarlet. I can't breathe without you." I kissed her then, nipping her bottom lip with my teeth.

"You're are one of the only people in this world that matters to me. I love you like I've never loved anything in my life." I backed her against the counter, my hands pushed into her hair while I planted kisses along her jaw. I needed her to know she was everything to me. I'd run to the ends of the earth to keep her safe and hold her in my arms.

"I love you too." Her hips arched against mine as the words tumbled out, the warmth charging through my heart with every syllable.

"You don't know what it does to me to hear you say that."

She sighed as I trailed a hand down her thigh, inching the hemline of her dress up.

"I'll spend a lifetime worshipping the ground you walk on." I pulled the dress over her head, revealing creamy skin to my love-drunk gaze. I lifted her small form onto the counter and peeled the cotton panties down her thighs. Heartbeats rioted in my chest at the sight of her silky, sweet pussy.

Trailing a single fingertip along the delicate skin of her mound, I lived for the shallow pants wracking her body in response to my touch. Her body was heaven on earth, the sweet moans falling from her lips like a siren song to my damaged heart.

"My beautiful, Scarlet." I praised as my eyes caught sight of the freshly baked cherry pie sitting on the counter. Plunging my fingers into the warm, oozing fruit, I dragged the confection across her sweet mound. Sugary sweetness painted her creamy skin and left my cock pounding underneath my pants.

"Fuck, I need you." I lapped at the cherry filling decorating her bare pussy before sliding another digit into the pie and smearing more across her breasts. Her hooded gaze caught mine as she watched me caress the soft treat across her nipple, coating it tenderly before my lips attached to it and sucked the pebbled peak clean. "I've been waiting a lifetime for you."

She mewled, and one palm fisted at the full flesh of her breast as I ran my fingers through her soaked flesh. "No more waiting, I'm yours, Beau."

Her words urged me on as my nostrils flared and I leaned over her body, my fingers smearing more red juice at her lips and down her neck, leaving a trail of the sticky-sweet residue for my tongue to follow. I kissed her fiercely, my tongue thrusting and tasting before I locked her arms above her head in one hand and sucked the rest of the cherry pie from her skin.

"You're a vision laid out for me like this. Look what you do to me." I pulled my thick cock from my pants and fisted it at the root.

With long strokes I pulled up and down the shaft, sliding the tip between her engorged pussy lips, teasing her entrance.

"I'll do anything to keep you with me tonight and every night after."

"You don't have to do anything, Beau. You are enough."

"Mm...*petite rouge.*" I wrapped my hands in her hair, sinking my hips between her thighs and pushing my swollen cock into her tight body. "I'm going to take this sweet pussy like a starved man. Not holding back anymore. I need you."

Her fingernails scraped across the bare flesh of my back as I pushed into her, the hot hum of her pussy clenching around my dick and reminding me why I'd driven all goddamn night to get here. Right here. Deep inside her, just where I needed to be.

Her back arched as I buried my cock deep inside her creamy body. My hands grazed up her skin, grabbing the round globes of her tits, then slid back down her curves as I savored the mewls sing-songing past her lips.

"You're an angel. Don't know how I lived a day without you." I caged her beneath me and pressed my lips to the hollow of her neck, sucking at the sweet flesh, feeling the delicate flutter of her heartbeat. She was my reason for waking up in the morning.

"Come for me, Red." I swirled my fingers at her sensitive clit, and her thighs gripped my waist, her fingernails searing the flesh at my back as she rode out her orgasm.

I stretched my palms across the hollow of her back and pulled her up to sit on my cock, the flex and pull of her pussy sending a crashing orgasm through my body. I held her fiercely as paths of fire shot through my muscles, wild, reckless lust fogging my brain.

"I missed you so much." I finally finished, my cock still pulsing deep inside her as I whispered against her neck.

"I missed you, too," she said drowsily into my shoulder. "Promise to never leave me again, deal?"

"No deal required, *petite rouge*. Wherever I go, you go. New rule."

"We have rules now?"

"Just the one." I gripped her delicious ass cheeks in my palms and rotated my hips, enjoying the feel of her sated body wrapped around my cock. "I don't have to worry about you disobeying, do I?"

"Mm…" A soft little moan escaped her throat. "No, Mr. Loup."

"Scarlet," I grunted, wrapping a hand around her neck and nipping at her lips in warning, my hips already rocking against hers as my cock twitched and flared back to full mast. "It's going to be a long night."

FIFTEEN

Scarlet

I woke the following morning to Beau's face nuzzling between my breasts, his tongue darting out between the heavy globes and tasting my skin like a delicacy.

"Mornin'," he whispered, as his heavy hands linked my wrists, stretching my arms above my head. Then he pulled a crimson ribbon from the side table and secured my wrists to the headboard.

"I'm having you for breakfast." His hands dove between my legs, spreading my thighs and causing all the air to vacate my lungs. "Love waking up with you." He kissed along my hips. "Love smelling this sweet pussy, wet for me anytime I want it." His eyes flashed, before his nose dusted across the crest of my mound, nestling between my swollen lips.

"You like that, baby? You like my eyes on you, my nose scenting you? I can't get enough. I want to sink my teeth into your flesh and mark you everywhere. I want my baby in your sweet belly. I want to tie you to me forever, Scarlet," he finished, and I barely had time to register his words before his tongue was lapping at my entrance. I curved and arched off the bed, my wrists pulling at my bindings as he ate me.

"God, Beau," I said incoherently as he sucked my clit between his lips and pulled. I groaned and ground my hips against his mouth, a release burning through my body. I bucked and panted, feeling his abrasive fingertips scrape across the sensitive skin at my waist. As I reached my peak, he flipped me over and caged me in.

His dick probed at my back entrance as arousal pulsed down my thighs.

"If you're on birth control, *petite rouge*, I want you off it. Starting now." He shoved in, bottoming out inside me on the first thrust and causing me to surge up the bed with the force of his passion.

I clutched at the headboard bars while his hands propped my hips in the air, digging into the flesh as he fucked me with hard, forceful thrusts. I moaned and whimpered, wishing desperately to have his wide body under my hungry hands.

"You want that, Scarlet? Want my babies deep inside you? Want me to spray your sweet pussy with my cum, knock you up and see you swollen with my babies?"

His words pummeled through my brain like a hurricane, mixing my need and lust for him into a heady concoction of intoxicated arousal.

"Yes, yes, Mr. Loup," I whimpered, knowing exactly what I'd done the moment I'd done it.

"Bad girl." The swift smack of his palm on my ass stung. I gritted my teeth, then wiggled my ass, feeling his cock seated deep inside me and hitting every engorged nerve I had. "Like making me angry, *petite rouge*?" He grinned and smacked my ass again, harder this time, but the sting was followed by the soft, gentle caress of his palm. The comfort seeped around my veins and into my heart left me at his mercy.

"Have me, anyway you want me. You can have it. You can have all of me," I uttered weakly as his palms slid across the dips and hollows of my body. His chest pressed against my back, his palms gripping my breasts as they swung against the bed sheets.

"That's what I wanted to hear." He nipped at the lobe of my ear before fisting my ass cheeks in his palms and beginning a fierce thrusting rhythm against me. I shuddered when one finger met my clit, as he pinched and swirled fiercely, the instant pain only relieved by the constant connection.

"Make me cum, *petite rouge*. Make me so fucking hot I spill my seed inside this sweet cunt, and you go home with my baby inside you."

Tears sprang against my eyelids as I rocked against his pelvis, my thighs clenching as I felt the fullness flexing inside me.

"That's it, fuck me, *petite rouge*." He bit me again, and I felt the quake of another orgasm take hold. His cock throbbed inside me as his hands gripped at my flesh, stretching and pulling my body, playing it like an instrument.

"Beau," I gasped as the orgasm burned through me, my mind lost in the pleasure. I felt his own violent thrusts shudder to a halt, his fingertips digging into my skin until I thought they might leave bruises.

"Love you, *petite rouge*. Love you so fucking much it makes my heart hurt," he said against my ear, resting on top of me, his hands unraveling the satin at my wrists, his thumbs working away any soreness. "Stay with me. Stay with me forever."

He flipped me over in his arms, his eyes intense with overwhelming emotions. He'd taken me, owned me since the first day he'd met me, consuming my thoughts and making me wild with need for him. His leaving the last few days to help his sister when she'd almost lost everything had only made me more sure of my feelings for him. He was loyal. A protector. Brave and strong and so gentle in his overbearing way, I loved him all the more.

"Yes. Always." Happy tears hovered at my eyelids as I tucked myself into the sheets with him, the morning sun burning up the air around us as we settled into our bubble once again. "I'll stay forever if you'll have me."

"Forever it is then." He placed a kiss on my nose before pulling me farther into the crook of his arm. "You and me, *petite rouge*, we start now."

SIXTEEN

Beau

The mid-summer sun rose high in the sky as June melted into July. Scarlet had been here for five weeks, and she'd been sneaking off to my place just about every night. We'd continued our affair underneath Ms. Fair's nose, but the time for telling was about to be upon us.

I'd known the day would come when we'd have to break it to Ms. Fair that Scarlet was mine and at the end of the summer she would not be leaving. She would be staying. *With me.*

Scarlet plopped her ass up on the bathroom vanity while I trimmed, cleaning up the scruff around my neck in the mirror. "Let's go swimming today."

I'd never get sick of having her here. The nights were better with her, and the days apart grew impossibly longer.

"You askin' me to play hooky?" I arched an eyebrow at her as I cleaned the scissors under the water and grabbed a towel.

"Play hooky with me, Mr. Loup." Her eyes flashed with seductive mischief.

"You're a bad influence." I winked, then looped the hand towel around her neck and pulled her to me. "Got a question for you."

"Mm, does it start with *will you* and end with *fuck me?*" Her eyes gleamed.

I laughed and shook my head, my grip loosening on

the towel. I pressed my forehead to hers. "There's something different about you. You're beautiful, you always are, but there's something else." I searched her face and sensed an energy radiating from her. "I know your body. I know you inside and out." My hands trailed down to her waist. "When's the last time you had your period, Scarlet?"

Her muscles tightened around me instantly, her gaze falling away from mine as her teeth worried her bottom lip.

"It's no big deal, just think about it. It's been over a month since you've been here…"

"I haven't had it since. But I'm sure I'm not, Beau. It's not like it happens the first time."

"The first time? We've had a hundred first times since then." I wrapped her in my arms. "Make ya a deal, I play hooky today, we stop by the store and pick up a pregnancy test, all right? Just to be sure?"

"Beau—"

"No arguing, *petite rouge*. I need to know." I shot her a warning glance, pressing my hands to her shoulder blades and massaging. "Need to take care of my woman and my baby if it's true."

"Fine." Her eyes turned to warm pools of emotion, and she wrapped her arms around my neck and pulled me in for a long, slow kiss. "I'll call the main house and let them know I'll be out all day."

We spent the day swimming at a lake not far away, and we'd had an astounding amount of privacy since it was the middle of the week. We both swam the shoreline, then ducked behind a large boulder and I finger-fucked her until she came so hard her eyes rolled back in her head. Never one to be outdone, she'd immediately returned the favor by slipping the elastic of her suit aside and impaling herself on my cock, riding me in the water until I shuddered and came with a grunt deep inside her. She was always taking my breath away and surprising me every single minute of the day.

After dining on French fries and cheeseburgers at the local diner, I pulled over at the pharmacy and put the truck in park, looking at her expectantly.

"This again?" she sighed, turning her gaze away. "I'm telling you, I'm perfectly fine. My periods have never been super regular."

"Don't kid yourself. I've been dumping my seed inside you every second I can. There's a good chance, Scarlet."

She heaved another sigh, then opened the door, launching herself out of my truck and taking off for the brightly lit double doors. I shook my head with a huff and followed her. She was a challenge, with that fiery personality rearing its beautiful head when I least expected it.

"This one okay?" she asked and thrust a little pink box in my face a minute later.

I crooked an eyebrow and took it from her, reading the back label before grabbing another box, then another. "These are good."

"Beau, you're crazy. Don't be impossible again." She pulled a box from my hand and set it back on the shelf.

"Bullshit. I need to know beyond a reasonable doubt." I swiped the little test back and made off down the aisle.

"Good evening." The cashier smiled brightly at us. We must have looked like quite the pair, my rough-around-the-edges ass next to her young, sweet doe-like eyes.

"Evenin'." I nodded and dumped the boxes on the

scanner. "We've got a bet." I winked at the cashier. Her eyes widened in surprise, but she didn't reply. "Guess we're gonna find out how potent the swimmers are." I caught Scarlet under my arm and pulled her close.

"You're just impossible. In all the really annoying ways." Scarlet grumbled and crossed her arms over her chest, shooting an apologetic smile to the cashier.

"Newlyweds?" The woman smiled at us.

"No," Scarlet replied just as I gave her a squeeze and said, "Yes."

Scarlet's eyes shot up to me, the blush burning up her cheeks and making me want to undress her and feast on her body all over again as soon as we got home.

"Cute. Best of luck." The cashier scanned the last box. "$36, please."

I swiped my card and then snagged the bag, holding Scarlet tightly with my other hand.

"I can't believe you spent $36 on tests for me to pee on," Scarlet teased as we walked out of the store.

I shook my head. "Now you're the one being impossible."

"Not as much as you. Not even close," she answered, then placed a kiss on the tip of my chin. "But thank you for being so thoughtful."

"It's damn more than that. I'll be taking care of both of you."

"You already take care of me."

"The day I stop taking care of you, Scarlet Fair, is the day I'm dead. You won't ever have to worry about that." I pressed my hands into her hair and took her in a kiss. I pressed her up against the door of my truck and thrust my tongue between her lips until we were both gasping for air.

"I love you, Beau," she sighed.

My heart was more full than it'd ever been.

"Love you too, sweetheart." I stroked her hair and pulled her against my chest, thankful for every second I had her in my arms.

"Beau!" she squealed when I lifted her in my arms and carried her through my house ten minutes later.

"Just trying to be helpful." I sat her down in the bathroom and hooked my thumbs in her panties.

"You're being a distraction right now! I need to focus," she laughed and gestured for me to turn around.

"Not a chance, baby. You're mine, and I'm yours. That means I have a right to your *everything*. Now sit… squat…do whatever you girls do…and go."

"But Beau…?" She paused, feeling a flip of dread turn my stomach. "What if it's positive? What if we're…"

"Hey, hey, hey." I cupped her face in my palms. "Whatever that little test says, nothing changes. What you and I have, we'll always have. That will last for eternity, I can promise you that, love. Don't worry 'bout a thing. I'll take care of all of us."

A slow smile crept across her lips. "I love you, Beau."

"Ahh, *petite rouge*, I loved you the first day you fell into my arms."

I swiped at a tear hovering in her eye. She heaved a big sigh before picking up the first box.

"No, this one first." I thrust another at her. "Looked better." I shrugged when her eyes widened in surprise. "Just sit."

"So impossible." She mouthed the words before she pulled her dress up and sat down. "Are you really going to watch me the whole time?"

"Oh, for God's sakes, piss on the stick, woman," I huffed.

She laughed, before replying, "Sorry, *Mr. Loup.*"

"And *I'm* the impossible one," I grunted and left the room, stopping just outside the door. Be damned if I was going to get a step farther away from her than I had to.

"I can't do it when you're hovering."

"You're doing it just fine. Relax." I peeked around the corner.

She arched an eyebrow back at me. "Do you have a doctor's degree I don't know about?"

My laugh filled the small space.

"There." She thrust the stick towards me with a charming smile.

I crossed the room in two strides and took the test from her. "Now we wait."

"Good luck. I'm surprised you're not going to threaten the damn thing to give you the results sooner." Scarlet finished up and flushed while I perched the test on top of its box.

"Smartass," I chided while we washed our hands. "You want something to eat? Are you thirsty? We need to make sure you're getting enough calories."

"Beau, I'm hardly pregnant."

"You could be. Two more minutes and we'll know for sure." I placed a kiss on her bare knuckles, a reminder that she wasn't officially bound to me yet, and instantly thought I needed to rectify that with something big and shiny soon.

"Counting down the minutes already? I'm a little afraid you'll be disappointed if it's negative."

I smiled, enjoying these moments with her. I hoped she was carrying my child, and someday we could tell the little him or her all about this moment when we first found out together. "It won't be negative, *petite rouge*. I know that as well as I know the curves of your body."

"Beau?" she said. I covered her word in a kiss.

"It's time," I said when I finished, my hands stroking her shoulders reverently.

"You look at it first. You tell me," she said as she quaked on nervous legs behind me.

I lifted the little white stick in my palm and squinted at the results. I flipped it over in my head, furrowing my forehead. "What do two pink lines mean again?"

"Beau!" she shrieked and swatted at my shoulder, swiping the test from my palms and reading the results for herself.

"Congratulations, mama." I pulled her into my arms, hauling her into the air and spinning her in the small space.

"Beau, how is it possible? The first month?!"

"I manage the impossible, remember?" I grinned, placing a kiss on her mouth, feeling what had now become that familiar feeling radiating between us. Love multiplied. It was the three of us now, and the little life growing inside her connected us on a whole new level.

"I can't believe we're going to have a baby. Maybe I should take another test. Do you think it could be wrong?" She pulled away, her eyes gleaming up at me, happiness pulsing from every pore.

"Yeah, baby. We'll do another one. But right now I just want you. Can't let you go just yet." I nuzzled into her hair, imbibing her gentle aura into my system.

"Let's take a bath. I need to take care of both of you."

SEVENTEEN

Scarlet

Hummingbirds flitted around in my stomach as I waited, Beau's hand pressed in mine, my legs shifting anxiously as we waited in the foyer.

"We have to tell them, right? Are you sure we can't just run away and never come back?"

"Ha, not a chance. I'm proud of the life we created. No chance in hell I'm running from it." He squeezed my hand in his.

"Okay." I swallowed the lump in my throat and smoothed the hem of my dress.

"Hey, I got you. No matter what happens, I got you." He caught my chin in his fingers and kissed me squarely on the lips.

"Stop, they might see." I squirmed with a smile, cognizant of the people waiting just around the corner.

"And I wouldn't give a fuck if they did. You are mine. We are a family now, whether they want to admit it or not. That's the bottom line."

"You don't know them. They won't hold back." Tears began a stubborn swell in my eyes.

"But I know you, and I know if they love you like I do, they wouldn't walk away. They'll do everything they can to support you."

I nodded, sucking in a breath and getting control of my roller-coaster emotions. Just another symptom of pregnancy, I'd read.

We'd wanted to do this the right way and had called my parents down for the weekend.

My parents were now sitting in the living room, sipping hot tea and chatting with Gran. They'd exchanged long, loving hugs, but I was secretly terrified that my and Beau's confession may bring up old feelings. I knew I needed to see them with Beau by my side, I wouldn't have the strength any other way. This would be so unexpected, I'd never even mentioned a crush to them before. The idea that I'd found the man I loved and we were ready to spend the rest of our lives together as we raised our baby would shock them.

"I'm ready." I clutched his hand in mine as we took the few steps around the corner and entered the elegant front sitting room of the manor.

"Scarlet!" my mother cried and shot up, running to me with open arms. "We've missed you so much."

My father joined us, and we all hugged. "It's so good to see you."

"You look healthier. This southern sun has done you well." Dad placed a kiss on my cheek.

"Thanks, Daddy. I missed you guys so much." I smiled. "Actually, I have someone I'd like you to meet."

"Oh, Beau! I'm so glad you're here!" Gran stood and rifled in the drawer she kept her gardening magazines in. "I saw this koi pond—"

"Actually, Gran, Beau is here for a different reason." I stepped back to his side, locking his hand in mine.

"He's my—"

"Fiancé. Beau Loup, nice to meet you." Beau stepped

forward to shake my parents' hands.

"Fiancé?" My mother's forehead furrowed as she looked from me to him and back again.

I nodded slowly before holding out my hand, the gleaming rock Beau had placed on it just last night now blinding in the morning sunlight.

"Scarlet!" my mother shrieked and held my hand up to hers as if checking the ring was real, then glared at Beau and Gran.

"How did this happen? John, can you believe this?" My mother turned to my father.

His dark eyes searched my face before seeking out Beau's. "Can I have a word, young man?"

Beau's eyes shot up, and he nodded, leaving the room with my father.

"Scarlet, what are you thinking?!"

Gran approached, one comforting palm trailing through my hair. I closed my eyes, taking comfort from her quiet demeanor.

"It happened when I wasn't looking. I met him one day and the next, I couldn't stop thinking of him. We kept bumping into each other, and when we're together, it's like the world rights itself. Everything is so messy and complicated, but all of it makes sense when I'm in his arms," I breathed, hoping they'd see through to the heart of me.

"Oh, Scarlet." My mother took me in her arms, hugging me fiercely.

"Love does funny things." Gran nodded before looking up to the doorway.

"Seems there's something else they'd like to tell us," my father said when he entered the room, pressing a kiss on my forehead as he passed.

"Mr. and Mrs. Fair. I'd like Scarlet to stay with me here. I know this place is special to her, and I'd like to raise our baby right here where I grew up."

My heart flip-flopped as he dropped our biggest revelation on them.

"Your baby?" My mother's eyes widened and shot to my belly.

"A baby, Mama. We're going to have a baby." I couldn't help the smile that spread my cheeks. I went to her, arms wide as we crushed each other in a tight hug.

"Oh, honey. I never wanted that for you." Tears hovered in her eyes, and I sensed she was remembering a time in the distant past, my father and her confessing the very same situation to Gran.

"I know what you wanted, Mama, but I'm happy here. I'm the happiest I've ever been." I clasped Beau's hand in mine and gazed up at him, love simmering in the gaze between us.

"I had no idea when you left, that the next time I'd see you, you'd be a woman." The words choked my mother's throat before a small smile turned at the corners of her lips.

"I had no idea either. Everything has taken me by surprise." I couldn't keep the grin from splitting my cheeks.

Mama slowly nodded. "I can see there's not a thing I can say to change your mind, and even if I did, it would be purely selfish on my part." My mother looked at Beau, then back to me. "Love. I could see it on you when you walked in. Happiness looks beautiful on you, sweetheart."

A few more happy tears trailed down my cheeks before I turned to my dad.

"We had a talk. As long as he takes care of you, I'm a happy man. Only the best for my little girl." He placed an emotional kiss on my forehead, then turned away, swiping at his eyes awkwardly.

"Thank you, Daddy."

"Your daddy and I used to dream about a wedding in the back garden. That didn't happen for us, but maybe, with Gran's blessing, it will for you." Mama cradled my cheek in her palm

"I would love that." I grinned up at Beau and saw his smile spread.

He pressed my hand to his lips and placed a kiss there. "I would marry you anywhere, Scarlet Fair, but right here feels just about perfect."

EIGHTEEN

Beau

By the time summer sun set on the last week of August, Scarlet had the slightest bump protruding at her waistline. She was mine.

Like every fiber in my body had been telling me the day we'd met, Scarlet was mine to keep, and today would only make it official.

Today Scarlet's father would walk her down the aisle and give her away.

To me.

I straightened my tie in the mirror, feeling, not for the first time, like the damn thing was choking me. I grunted, then spun, knocking over a photo of my parents. I sucked in a breath of air that actually stung on the way in. It pained me that they weren't here, would never get the chance to meet the beautiful woman who had captivated my heart. Marrying Scarlet was a dream come true. Our courtship had happened in such a rush, our circumstances certainly not average, but we'd found love just the same. I only wished they could be here to share it all with us, but I was certain they would be here in spirit.

We'd thought about postponing the wedding for my sister, but she was still completing her ninety days in rehab, stronger and healthier than ever, and had plans to move into a transitional house after finishing. She'd wished us well and promised that she would come to visit soon, but that she didn't feel strong enough to be exposed to all the temptations of the outside world just yet. I'd been silently saddened, but knew she was taking the right steps in her recovery and for that I was prouder of her than ever.

I turned back to the mirror, adjusted my tie once more, then flicked off the lights and left. I had a wedding to get to.

Taking long strides down the driveway, I cut left to head down the path that led to the big house. I stopped when I came to the tree line, taking in the massive estate. The mansion looked stately in the background, the rolling green gardens and terraces were always breathtaking, but now, in the evening light, even more so. Rows of chairs decorated the lawn, a large white tent to feed our guests after, and one long aisle. People milled around. A grand piano had been set up on the patio, and a pianist released sweet chords into the air.

It was a fairy tale, without a doubt. But my real happily ever after was getting Scarlet. I hadn't seen her coming, was powerless in the face of the control she held over me, and utterly bewitched by everything that was her. Scarlet had chosen me, and I'd spend every day of my life proving to her that she'd made the right choice.

I walked the remaining yards down the path to the gardens, where I would take my spot at the end of the aisle as the groom. I approached Scarlet's grandmother, and she welcomed me in a hug. She'd grown frailer as the months of summer had gone on. Scarlet was worried, and that was part of the reason why we'd wanted to rush the wedding, so we could share this day with her.

"You're such a wonderful, kind man, Beau." She patted me on the cheek. "I know somewhere deep in that stubborn heart of yours, you probably don't think you deserve her, but you deserve all the love she has for you. You deserve everything, Beau."

"Ms. Fair, you brought me Scarlet, and for that, I can't thank you enough." I held my arms open, and the little old woman tucked herself against my body.

"This summer has been nothing short of magic. I'm an old woman. I won't be around for much longer, but I wanted to give you this." She handed me an envelope. "It's my will. I'm leaving you and Scarlet the house. I've always wondered who would live here after I was long gone, but now I can rest happy knowing it will stay in the family."

"No ma'am." I shook my head. "I don't think we can accept that. It's too generous."

"Nonsense. Scarlet is my granddaughter, and the only other person I would consider leaving it to is standing right before me." She smiled. "Now I don't want to make you late on your big day. Go get your girl."

"Thank you, ma'am." I nodded, and she smiled and turned away, walking back to her seat in the front row. There's another woman who constantly took me by surprise. Maybe it ran in the family.

Scarlet's mom sat next to Ms. Fair and an empty chair where Scarlet's dad would soon be sitting. My eyes crossed the aisle to the handful of people I'd invited, all the chairs filled except for two in the front row. A bouquet of white lilies on both in honor of my parents. It'd been Scarlet's idea to include them, and the idea touched me to the very core of my heart. It was perfect.

The music started then, and I took my place at the head of the aisle beneath the flowering trellises, waiting for my girl.

Finally, the music changed, and Scarlet and her dad

turned the corner and began their slow march down the aisle. My eyes were riveted the entire journey, my gaze caressing her form as she walked to me, tears shimmering in her eyes and a smile hovering on her lips.

"*Petite rouge*, you look edible." My voice was husky as she clung to my arms. "I want to peel this fluffy white confection off your body and taste you."

A vibrant shade of red climbed up her cheeks before the cleric cleared his throat and started. I tuned out his words, my eyes only focusing on Scarlet's.

"Who gives this woman?" I heard him ask, and her father stepped forward. "I do."

The ceremony continued. We recited our vows and were finally pronounced man and wife. When he said the words, I took her face in my palms and kissed her like no one was watching.

"Love you so much," I nipped at her earlobe.

"I love you too." Her smile lit up my entire fucking world.

"Ladies and gentleman, Mr. and Mrs. Loup."

Scarlet's eyes twinkled when she locked hands with mine, and we walked down the aisle, man and wife, the first day of our forever.

After a delicious catered dinner, Scarlet and I headed for the dance floor for our first dance. I wrapped her in my arms and tucked my nose into her shoulder as the first few chords of 'You Belong to Me' started.

"Beau, this song…it's your mother's song." She stopped for a moment once she recognized it.

I nodded and pulled her back to me. "It's the perfect song. You gave me life, Scarlet. I don't know what I would do without your love." I pulled her even tighter to me as the song continued. "You're my dream. The dream I didn't even know I was wishing for."

"I love you so much," she whispered and pressed up on her toes to kiss me.

"I'd be so alone without you." I murmured the words of the song. "You belong to me. I'll love you every day of forever, *petite rouge*."

EPILOGUE

Scarlet

One year later

The Saturday morning sun glinted off the treetops as I sat swinging on the front porch of our cabin.

"Need anything, babe?" Beau hurried out and dropped a kiss on my cheek.

"Lemonade maybe? It's going to be hot today." I scrunched my nose. "Will you grab the sunscreen, too?"

Beau ran back into the cabin and returned a minute later with both.

"What do you say we go up to the big house today, see how renovations are coming?"

"That sounds great. I'll probably have to pee three times before we get there though," I grumbled, already feeling uncomfortable.

"Ah, tell Mama she's got another seven months to go," Beau chuckled and pulled our squirming son into his arms.

"I'm not complaining, but this heat makes it worse!" I tickled Ben's toes, and he broke into a gummy grin.

"You gotta be the little man around the house while I'm gone." Beau tickled him, and a few giggles escaped his belly.

"I can't believe we're going to have two kids under two." I rubbed at my still mostly flat belly.

"We've been busy, Mama." Beau winked at me.

"I just wish Gran was here to see them." Sadness creeped crept into my thoughts.

"She can see them just fine. I know she's watching over both of them." He cradled Ben in one arm and placed another on my shoulder.

"Let's go for that walk now. I want to make sure the builders are on top of it."

Gran had passed away in her sleep just six weeks after we were married. When Beau had told me she'd left us the house, I nearly crumbled into tears. Her generosity and kindness were so overwhelming, I was instantly overcome by the realization that my kids would never have the privilege of knowing her.

At first, I hadn't wanted to even see the house, Beau and I having decided early on that we wanted to live in the cabin at the back of the property. I'd never grown up with excess. I preferred a simple quieter life, and the thought of all that room in the mansion going to waste had nagged at me.

After talking it over many late nights with Beau, we finally settled on a boarding house for underprivileged new moms. Whether they were pregnant, or had just had their baby, we would welcome them into the main house for as long as they needed, and provide them with resources and training to get back on their feet.

I think Gran would be happy with what we'd decided to do with her home.

We followed the path of the morning sun as we walked the trail to the main house. Beau lifted Ben onto his shoulders and held his chubby hands as we walked, his little green eyes wide with wonder at the world around him.

It was an amazing place, and we were so blessed to call it home.

Life was good. Life had given me the fairy tale. I'd

never imagined that I would go away for the summer and become a new woman. I never imagined I'd find my soul mate, and he would be six-two with a beard and a rakish grin. I never dreamed of the beautiful little boy with the vibrant green eyes and strawberry-red hair.

They'd given me so much love every day. I only wanted to give it back, share it, multiply it until every life we touched was painted in vibrant brushstrokes of compassion, empathy, and tenderness.

Beau gave me everything, and I would live out the remainder of my days giving all my love back to him.

THE END.

Acknowledgments

First, I have to thank my ever so loving and patient husband. You truly are my HEA, babe. <3

Thank you to Aria's Assassins for keeping my fire burning. I am forever grateful for your love and cheerleading!

I can't thank the ArdentProse team enough. You ladies make my life so much easier and I love you for it!

To my ladies...the ladies that love to get lost in books about true and last lasting love... THANK YOU!!! Writing books you love is what keeps me going. You are my rock stars!

About the Author

Aria Cole is a thirty-something housewife who once felt bad for reading dirty books late at night, until she decided to write her own. Possessive alpha men and the sassy heroines who love them are common, along with a healthy dose of irresistible insta-love and happily ever afters so sweet your teeth may ache.

For a safe, off-the-charts HOT, and always HEA story that doesn't take a lifetime to read, get lost in an Aria Cole book!
Follow Aria on Amazon for new release updates, or stalk her on Facebook and Twitter to see which daring book boyfriend she's writing next!

More from Aria Cole:

Black
Swan
White
Scarlet
Bending Bethany
Chasing Charlie

 Sign up to get a NEW RELEASE ALERT from me!
→ http://eepurl.com/ccGnRX

.